SHE CAME TO CON [barcode] D0361675

When Althea agreed to introduce her _____ ___ to London Society, she never suspected she would face such a devilishly difficult challenge.

Before she met Lucy, she imagined she would have to protect this inexperienced Miss raised in distant India from the dangers and designs of unscrupulous gentlemen.

But when this extraordinarily beautiful and exceptionally calculating young creature arrived, Althea discovered her task would be far different.

She did not have to protect Lucy from gentlemen, she had to protect gentlemen from Lucy—especially the one particular gentleman who made Althea lose both her temper and her heart. . . .

The
Unruly Bride

More Delightful Regency Romances from SIGNET

The
Unruly Bride

by

Vanessa Gray

A SIGNET BOOK

NEW AMERICAN LIBRARY

NAL BOOKS ARE AVAILABLE AT QUANTITY DISCOUNTS WHEN USED
TO PROMOTE PRODUCTS OR SERVICES. FOR INFORMATION PLEASE WRITE
TO PREMIUM MARKETING DIVISION, NEW AMERICAN LIBRARY,
1633 BROADWAY, NEW YORK, NEW YORK 10019.

SIGNET TRADEMARK REG. U.S. PAT. OFF. AND FOREIGN COUNTRIES
REGISTERED TRADEMARK—MARCA REGISTRADA
HECHO EN CHICAGO, U.S.A.

SIGNET, SIGNET CLASSIC, MENTOR, PLUME, MERIDIAN AND NAL
BOOKS are published by New American Library,
1633 Broadway, New York, New York 10019

First Printing, February, 1985

1 2 3 4 5 6 7 8 9

PRINTED IN THE UNITED STATES OF AMERICA

1

Althea Rackham, always susceptible to beauty, paused on her way home to admire yet again the perfect arrangement of buildings and streets that had sprung from the brain of Thomas Nash, architect. She wondered whether she would ever tire of the warm golden stone, the towers of the abbey—now, of course, the product of Mr. Nash.

She had taken a house in Laura Place because Mary Benbow—a distant relation and her lifelong friend and, since the past two years her companion—had fallen ill of a congestion, and it was felt that the waters of Bath would be beneficial.

Now she was on her way home from Meyler & Sons bookstore in Milsom Street. She carried two books just published, and while they would not have been her own choice, yet Bennie might beguile her tedious invalid's hours with them.

Bath would be delightful, she thought, were it not for the residents—at least the temporary ones. It seemed that all of society had come to fit themselves for the strenuous social Season just ahead. There was not a house for hire, she had been told only that morning, so great was the press of visitors.

And, she saw with some dismay, one of the less interesting of them was now approaching. If there had been time, she would have turned abruptly into a side street, hoping he had not seen her. There was not the slightest chance of escape, for Mr. Milburn—as he told her often—was excessively farsighted.

She greeted him with every appearance of civility. "Good afternoon, Mr. Milburn." She took her gloved hand from her muff and offered it.

He bowed over it. "I am most fortunate in meeting you, Miss Rackham. I have just called at your house. I was perturbed to learn you were walking abroad alone."

"Pinkham is coming along behind me," said Althea, and then flushed with vexation. She had no need to explain her actions to anyone, particularly Mr. Milburn, whom she was learning to dislike. Indeed, if he offered once again for her, she would tell him, more firmly this time, that there was no use for him to hope to wed her. Her gentle refusals had, so far, had little effect on him.

Mr. Milburn was not above the average in height, and his shoulders were broad, giving him a less-than-elegant appearance. He made up for his lack, however, by a meticulous and costly attention to his wardrobe. His black coat and light pantaloons were sober enough, but his gold-figured waistcoat hinted that he was at heart a dandy.

"I shall offer my escort," he said, turning his face toward Laura Place, "inasmuch as your maid is not yet within view."

Althea glanced over her shoulder. Pinkham had stopped to execute some errands and must have been delayed. However, relief was in sight.

"Sir Horace is coming this way," she said. "It would be most discourteous not to wait for him."

There was a touch of mischief in her smile. She was well aware that Mr. Milburn considered Sir Horace his greatest rival in the contest for the hand of Althea Rackham—and, she suspected in the case of Mr. Milburn, for her fortune.

They waited in silence for Sir Horace Wychley, the last of a respectable line of barons, a line that was

clearly dwindling. Sir Horace was not possessed of
great intelligence, nor wit. Neither, however, was he
demanding or in any way uncomfortable. Besides,
Althea had a strong suspicion that his devotion to the
inhabitants of the house in Laura Place was not im-
partial. At least, he was infinitely patient and untiring
with Bennie. Althea was greatly pleased to see him.

Sir Horace arrived. Ignoring Mr. Milburn, he smiled
at Althea. "Always a delight, dear Miss Rackham.
May I escort you?"

"She has an escort," said Mr. Milburn testily.

"Ah," said Sir Horace, looking at him as though just
now aware of his presence.

Sensing the restiveness of Mr. Milburn and Sir
Horace's scarcely hidden contempt for him, Althea
intervened. "I shall not stir a step without both of you.
I cannot think what can have happened to Pinkham.
But it is much too chilly to stand, and I confess I long
for a fire and a dish of tea."

She had begun to walk as she was talking, and with a
quick step each of the gentlemen caught her up. She
continued a gentle stream of civil remarks, and eventually the trio arrived at her door.

Essentially modest, she was at a loss to understand
her attraction for Mr. Milburn. She knew she was not a
beauty. Her mouth, for example, was wide enough to
be called generous, and her hair, of a particularly un-
distinctive shade of brown, was too fine to lend itself to
most of the intricate fashions of the day. In truth,
though Pinkham struggled mightily, Althea usually
had it dressed à la Ninon, with a simple riband woven
through it.

She was not aware of the effect of her very expres-
sive gray eyes, moving quickly from mischief to
sympathy and, most often, to amusement. None of
these was particularly useful in the Marriage Mart,
and indeed, she had quite given up thought of com-
peting again in the endeavor to marry. She was nearly
twenty-three years of age, and her betrothal—broken

in a spectacular and, she had to admit, unedifying manner two years since—had blasted any hopes she might have in the direction of marriage.

She was, she told herself often, content with her life, and would be completely happy if Bennie were well again.

When Althea entered her parlor, her two escorts behind her, she found Bennie huddled over the fire.

"Bennie, I had quite expected to find you secluded in your room. Does this mean you feel better?"

Bennie greeted the gentlemen before she answered. "I do believe those drafts are doing me some good. It is well understood, is it not, that if medicine tastes pleasant, it cannot be efficacious?"

"In that case," Althea said, "I should not be surprised to see you dancing in the Assembly Rooms in a fortnight."

Settled with dishes of bohea for the ladies, and sherry for the gentlemen, they began to talk of the coming Season in London.

"Parliament will be in session until June, I am told," said Mr. Milburn, "and it is incumbent upon us all to maintain a close supervision over its actions. I cannot quite like the prospect of the Duke of Wellington in the cabinet, as I have been assured he will be. I do not trust the military."

"Let the fellows alone," recommended Sir Horace. "You get a fanatic along one line"—he gave Mr. Milburn a hard stare that placed him, in Sir Horace's opinion, in the front line of fanaticism—"and you'll get one just as addled on the other side. Balances out every time."

Mr. Milburn gathered himself visibly together to enter the lists, but fortunately the arrival of visitors deflated him.

Lord Hatton, a man quite in the shade of his vivacious gossipy wife, followed his lady into the room. Exclamations were made over Bennie's convalescence, and Lady Hatton, a small woman with dark hair and a quick jerky way with her head, seemed even more bird-like than usual as she darted to Bennie's chair and tugged at the blankets.

Althea thought, I simply must get hold of myself. I am becoming quite foolish—imagine thinking Lady Hatton resembles a diligent robin tugging at a worm, when all she is doing is making Bennie comfortable. A glance at Bennie's face, however, did not reassure her as to the invalid's comfort.

At length Lady Hatton sat down, accepted a dish of tea from Tyson, and settled back in her chair. "I declare that Bath is quite the most deserted backwater in England. There is simply nothing going on!"

"But the Assembly Rooms were crowded even this morning when Bennie and I went. I left her in the Pump Room, you know, drinking those noxious drafts, and strolled through the rooms. There was hardly a chair empty at the card tables, and as for sitting down for refreshment, it was quite impossible."

"Oh, that!" Lady Hatton dismissed a hundred important people with a wave of her hand. "I mean exciting things. But then, we shall all be in London quite soon. We ourselves are leaving Friday week for Green Street."

Lord Hatton's attempts to share his wife's predilection for gossip were well-known. Unfortunately, he often missed the mark and relayed with every appearance of confidentiality tidbits that had long been common currency among the knowledgeable. Today, however, he had not said a word, and Althea had all but forgotten his presence.

Suddenly he spoke, and she turned, startled. "What's that Miss Morton up to, that's what we all want to know?"

"Isobel Morton?" asked Althea. Miss Morton, the perennially hopeful belle of London, a couple of years older than Althea, and therefore past the fateful age of twenty-five—yet still eager, willing, and obviously ready to accept any offer that came her way.

Althea would have inquired further. She could not quite sort out the right words. It would be unkind to say, "Who is she after this year?" But that, or a variation of that theme, was all that came to her mind.

Before she could discipline her unruly thoughts, she caught Lady Hatton's fiery eye firmly on her husband. Even from where Althea sat, she could translate the message.

Lord Hatton said, "Yes, you know she's making a success of it this time. Most remarkable because—" He had received his wife's message and sputtered to a stop.

Althea's curiosity was spurred. She opened her lips to demand further information, but the embarrassed expression on Lord Hatton's flushed face begged her not to proceed. Instead, she smiled and turned the conversation.

Before the Hattons could take their leave, two more visitors arrived.

"Oh," exclaimed Lady Hatton, stretching to look through the window at the ladies on the top step. "It's the Burrell women. Come, George, we must go at once. Miss Lydia is not so bad, but I have never known any gossip as vicious as Miss Jenny. On second thought, my dear," she added, addressing Althea, "I think we shall stay, since it is better to hear firsthand what they say about one rather than turn one's back. Sit down, George."

But today's burden of gossip carried by the Misses Burrell was insignificant. Indeed, Althea thought they were somewhat taken aback to see the other visitors. That impression was strengthened by their departure after a short time. When they had gone, the others, relaxing as a fox might when the hunt had swept on out of sight, began to move toward departure.

The words Lady Hatton spoke to Althea were the most unsettling of the afternoon. "Whatever they tell you," she said in a tone designed not to reach the others, milling near the open front door, "don't believe it. She could not be so fortunate." Without another word, Lady Hatton swept out of the house.

Unsettling, yes—and puzzling in the extreme. "She?" "Fortunate?" Althea was not averse to speculating about the activities of anyone she knew. Since she was very well connected, and popular with every London hostess, her acquaintance was wide and, within the limits of society, varied. Indeed, if one refused to listen to even the most harmless gossip, one might as well turn hermit and embrace the solitary life. After all, what else was there to do?

Back in the parlor, she and Bennie were at last alone, in the comfortable companionship experienced by every family when guests have departed. Althea rang for hot tea.

"What do you think Isobel Morton is up to?" Althea said after Tyson had brought the tea and left. "I know if his wife had not been here, Lord Hatton would have told us the whole. I suppose she is receiving attentions that as usual she elevates into a veritable offer."

Bennie was occupied with her tea and did not answer. She was eleven years older than Althea and a pleasant-looking woman when she was well. Without fortune of her own, she was dependent upon other more prosperous relations, an existence in which most happiness must be only vicarious. On the fringe of events, she managed well, possessed as she was of a sweet undemanding disposition, a large supply of gratitude for which she had frequent need, and an ability to turn her hand to a variety of tasks.

When Althea had come into her fortune two years ago and set up her own household, she had sent for Bennie to come as chaperone, companion, but mostly as friend.

"I have never liked Isobel," Althea mused, "for she seems to me to be completely selfish."

Bennie set her cup down. "My dear, each of us is selfish in one way or another."

"Everyone but you," said Althea affectionately.

"I hope I have overcome such a detestable vice." She fell silent, as though turning something over in her mind, before continuing. "Althea, you must know there is no place like the Pump Room for gossip. Some of it, indeed, is as noxious as that odoriferous water."

Althea watched her friend with growing uneasiness. Some uncertainty in Bennie's manner, perhaps the unusual restless movement of her hands in her lap, hinted at surprise to come.

"And gossip can be so dreadfully hurtful! But I am persuaded, my dear, you will not suffer the slightest tinge of unhappiness. I know, and every day I am grateful anew, that you have put that unfortunate business behind you." She lifted her gaze to meet Althea's gray eyes and gave her the ineffably sweet smile that came from her heart. "In fact, dear Althea, I am so convinced of your recovery on that head that I have been expecting an interesting announcement at any moment."

"An announcement—from me? Bennie, pray explain your meaning, for I am quite baffled."

"Mr. Milburn, you know. He is so assiduous in his attentions that I feel sure you must have given him some encouragement."

"Mr. Milburn," said Althea with spirit, "may go— Sometimes I wish I were a man. Being female sadly inhibits one's powers of expression."

"Then, dear, you do not mean to have him?"

"Certainly not."

"Then—I do not mean to be critical, you know—but do you not think he should be told his suit cannot prosper?"

"I inform him of that fact weekly. His understanding is not strong, I must assume, else why would he think we could ever suit? The man's a gadfly!"

In the ensuing silence, Althea had time to reflect on Bennie's conversation. The matter to which she referred could not be mistaken. At length, she ventured, "By 'that unfortunate business,' I must believe you mean Lord Soames?" Bennie's compassionate expression told her she had hit the mark. Stoutly, Althea told her, "I certainly have recovered from that—that near disaster. I cannot think how I could ever have been attracted to him. He is possessed of an arrogance that outrages all decency!" In a moment, in an altered tone, she added, "I myself, I believe, am not precisely biddable."

With unexpected irony, Bennie murmured, "Do you say so!"

Althea ignored her remark. "And certainly Simon Halleck—I should say Lord Soames now—has as strong a temper as any man outside a Minerva novel."

She paused, remembering that quarrel, the last and final one of many that she and Simon had had throughout their passionate—and brief—betrothal.

She had gone over every word they had spoken, over and over for weeks, even after the notice of the broken engagement had appeared in the *Gazette*. It was not particularly satisfying to realize that she could not remember the initial issue of the quarrel, but only its ramifications, which had ranged over a wide variety of subjects—those, and the harsh wounding words and the unjust accusations, on both sides.

Surely the fact that she could not remember the cause proved that she was emotionally whole again? Or perhaps only that she remembered other things better: his arms around her, his demanding lips on hers, the promise in his eyes.

She looked up, aware of Bennie's concerned watchfulness. "I gather, Bennie, that your time in the Pump Room this morning was not entirely occupied with the medicinal drafts? You may as well tell me what you heard about Isobel Morton. The gossip may amuse me." And I certainly need diverting, she added to herself.

With obvious reluctance, Bennie told her. "Lord

Soames—yes, dear, *your* Lord Soames—is in London,
after two years' rustication. It is said that he is hanging out for a wife.''

Althea was stunned. In a strangled tone, she
managed to say, "Simon, looking for a wife?"

Bennie nodded. "He is seen everywhere with—"

"Isobel Morton? Surely not! I would not expect him
to be satisfied with—with cold porridge!'' Especially
when she remembered that one of the side issues of the
final quarrel had dealt exhaustively with the subject of
Simon Halleck's sponsorship of a certain notorious
member of the muslin company and his adamant
refusal to give her up upon his marriage. "A namby-
pamby with the wit of a peahen!''

Bennie viewed the results of her plain speaking with
misgivings. "You did ask me to tell you the *on-dit*, my
love, and I have. Miss Morton is not quite as witless as
you think—'' She paled suddenly, with the fatigue of
the invalid that comes so swiftly and without warning.

"Bennie!'' cried Althea, springing up.

In a few moments Tyson was dispatched for maids
and a hot drink, and Bennie, supported by Pinkham,
Molly, and Samuel the footman, was taken upstairs
and put to bed with a brick at her feet.

In the confusion, and driven off by Althea's fears for
Bennie, Isobel Morton and even Simon himself were
forgotten.

At least for the moment.

2

Late March in Bath runs a gamut of weather. The previous day, while chilly, had been fair. This morning Althea awoke to lowering skies and pending storm.

The cup-shaped valley of the Avon held a full-to-overflowing measure of mist pressing up against the small windows of the house like a woolly shawl. The gloom thus induced in the breakfast room was matched by Althea's mood, the result of troubled dreams after she finally fell asleep.

Bennie, she was informed, was well enough this morning to have already ordered her breakfast, and later, in time for her daily journey to the baths, she would dress. In time, thought Althea darkly, to pick up another parcel of vicious gossip!

Essentially fair-minded, Althea put no blame on Bennie for telling her about Isobel and Simon. Such a mismated pair! It should be obvious to anyone that Simon would be mad to think he could not do better—

Althea felt a flush of shame warm on her cheeks. These were the sparse arguments that had kept her awake until nearly dawn. Not only were they ungenerous, but in the end, self-defeating. If Simon and Miss Morton were to make a match of it, it was no concern of hers. She was indeed recovered from the devastating blow of two years ago, and in that case, she did not care what Simon did. If she were not, then she had better work with diligence on the cure.

She was so wrapped up in her morose reflections that she did not at first realize that Tyson was hovering with more than his usual assiduity. No sooner had she emptied her cup when coffee reappeared, steaming, in it. Hot toast seemed to be in never-ending supply. And, she noted at last, Tyson was clearly possessed of information he wished to share. The curious inward look in his slate-colored eyes, as though to check that whatever his outer bearing concealed was still safely stored in his mind, gave an impression similar to a bottle of yeasty liquid. After yesterday's news—if such an unlikely rumor could be so dignified—she was not sure she wished to listen to her butler.

But it was likely that he had in mind only some aberration on the part of a member of her household staff, so it was without apprehension that she said, finally, "What is it, Tyson?"

"Thank you, miss. Cook desires me to inquire, Are Lord and Lady Darley to be expected for luncheon?"

Althea stared at him, amazed. "My brother and sister-in-law are at Darley Hall, Tyson," she said. One had always been told to treat carefully the infirm of mind. But suddenly she realized that Tyson seemed much as usual. She inquired suspiciously, "Why do you ask?"

"It is my custom, miss, to stand for a few moments upon the front step before locking the house for the night. A few moments of contemplation, miss, if I may so put it. Last night, I stood a few moments longer than is my habit, because it was then beginning to come on to rain." He paused, enjoying the suspense he was creating. Only a minatory glare from his mistress spurred him on. "A coach and four came into the street, followed by another, larger vehicle. And I am certain I saw the Darley crest on the panels."

Skeptical, she protested. "In the dark, Tyson?"

"The coach lamps, miss," he explained reproachfully. "And I am, of course, perfectly familiar with the family device."

"Of course," murmured Althea, puzzled in the extreme. What could Tom and Caroline be doing in Bath, unless one of them had become suddenly ill? She would have heard, in that case.

She was fond of her brother, especially when contemplating him as firmly installed no closer than Darley Hall, near Naunton Beauchamp. He had a strong bent toward authority, and since Althea was some years the younger, she had borne the burden. His marriage to Caroline Cathcart, the daughter of the Earl of Evesham, had done nothing to ease Althea's inferior position in the household, since Caroline was more inclined to instruct than to take instructions.

Fortunately—at least for Althea—an uncle had died suddenly, and to everyone's surprise he had bequeathed his London house, in Grosvenor Square, and a substantial income as well, to Althea. The legacy had been most timely, for she had just quarreled with Simon, and Caroline's opinion, fully and frequently expressed, of Althea's folly was particularly galling.

Now, while she could not welcome her brother and sister-in-law to her quiet circle of intimates, at least she could treat with them, if not precisely as an equal, at least not quite as a dependent.

Althea, seeing the butler waiting, said, "I shall not say you were mistaken, Tyson, but I have had no notice of their intentions." And I seriously doubt, she thought, that they have come to Bath.

Bennie planned to stay in her room until time to be driven again to the baths. She was certainly recovering her usual good health, but Althea was convinced that a winter in the Mediterranean climate would be beneficial.

Althea moved around her small parlor, too restless to settle to any occupation. She picked up the new issue of *Blackwood's* and dropped it. The anonymous writer who signed himself "Waverley" had written a new romance, *The Heart of Midlothian*, and she sat down to read it. She had reached the tenth page before she realized that she did not remember a word of what she had read.

At length, she isolated the real cause of her restlessness. She could not—quite simply—abide the thought of seeing Simon in town over the next few weeks.

Simon? Not so. It was the vision of Simon together with Isobel that galled her. To tell the truth, she thought in an orgy of jealousy—Simon and anybody. While she could not precisely attain the philosophy of "good riddance," yet she had thought herself heartwhole again. The emotions of the last eighteen hours had completely undeceived her on that head.

The suggestion of a winter in the Mediterranean was now as good as a promise in Althea's mind. If, as seemed now likely if rumor were true, the next months might well see Simon's marriage, she could discipline her emotions better from a distance.

Portugal perhaps, or Italy, whatever Napoleon's troops had left of it. She and Bennie would stay here in Bath throughout the summer, a period perhaps enlivened by a month at Darley Hall. Tom might well open the Dower House for them.

At that moment, Tyson threw open the parlor door. With a swift glance of triumph at his mistress, he announced, "Lord Darley."

Her brother burst into the room. He was a ruddy man above the average height, appearing to be more at home riding over his broad and prosperous acres than in a lady's salon, particularly one as minuscule as this one. Not bothering to lower his voice, he boomed, "What's the matter with Tyson? I told him he needn't bother to announce me. Man's a fool. How are you, Althea? Look not quite up to snuff to me." Without waiting for an answer, he went on, "Had an idea you'd still be here."

"Where else would I be?"

"London, of course, in that house Uncle Rackham

left you." A sudden thought struck him. "You're not taking the waters?"

"No, I wrote to Caroline that Bennie's not the thing."

"Good. The stuff is foul. Mama brought me here once when I was ten. Still taste it."

Skirting any tendency on her brother's part toward reminiscence, she said, "When did you arrive? Why didn't you let me know your plans? Is Caroline with you? Is she ill? I am persuaded you are quite healthy."

"It's Caroline. Wants to take the waters. A course of treatment, her quack tells her, before the summer."

To his sister's knowledgeable eye, Tom was not at ease. "A good idea," she agreed warily. "The London whirl is strenuous enough to daunt the most hardy."

Tom picked up *The Heart of Midlothian*, looked accusingly at it, and said, "Can't see what they see in this fellow. Just a story. Not a word of truth in the whole thing." He dropped the book onto the table. "Not going to London."

"Who isn't? Waverley?"

"Caroline. We're staying at Darley."

Althea was surprised. "Indeed? Tom, please sit down. You're pacing again, and while you're accustomed to the spaciousness of the rooms at Darley Hall, you must realize that my parlor is too small for your great strides." Returning to the subject at hand, she inquired, "Why not? Caroline always enjoys the Season."

"Can't leave the children."

Althea was jolted into indiscretion. "Fustian! Caroline has *always* left the children when it suited her."

Indeed, thought Althea, informed by her country upbringing, Caroline considered her children, when she thought of them at all, in the manner of a cowbird, which lays eggs in some other bird's nest, certain that, whoever reared the young, it would not be their mother.

Nurses and in due course governesses could do the
job, and Caroline would be well content.

Aloud, Althea said, "Odd. I had never believed Caroline to be a particularly doting mother." She was
struck by a sudden possibility. "Is she increasing
again?" So far, Caroline had produced four daughters
in quick succession, but not as yet an heir.

Tom sat down at last. He leaned forward, his hands
loosely together between his knees, the picture of
puzzled and, in a way, lonely bewilderment. He raised a
haunted face to her. "No. She's not. Says—you won't
credit me in this, but I swear it's true—says she wants
a rest. A *rest!*" He regarded his hands as though he
had never seen them before. "And by God, that's what
she's getting!" he added in a savage tone. "I shan't
touch her. Begging your pardon. Not fit subject."

Now she was beginning to understand. While she
had no experience in such matters—and would quite
likely never have—she could well imagine that four
confinements in five years might well suggest a "rest."
The cause of Tom's apparent wretchedness was
becoming clear.

Yet, watching the brother she knew so well, she perceived that he was laboring under strong emotion. She
was certain the half had not been told her. She was
about to ring for refreshments in the hope that wine
might loosen Tom's tongue.

Suddenly he blurted, "How much do you remember
about Edward?"

She was astounded. By paternal edict, since his
departure, her brother Edward's name had not been
spoken in the family during their father's lifetime. By
the time old Lord Darley had died, leaving title and
estates to his elder son, Thomas, Edward had been forgotten, at least by Althea.

Swiftly calculating, she said, "Just that he died over
a year ago. It's been almost twenty years, Tom. I was
only five years old."

Tom nodded. "I know. But I thought you might remember something. Bennie was there when it all happened.''

When what happened? When Tom went on, she realized she had not spoken aloud. "He was always wild, but I never thought— He must have been so bitter all those years, you'd think he would at least have . . .''

His voice trailed away. Clearly he was overcome by his emotion. In truth, she thought there might even be tears standing in his eyes. He kept his gaze averted, and she could not be sure. At length, he mumbled, "Dammit, I still miss him!''

Althea reviewed her limited knowledge. Tom was a year older than Edward, so they must have been close. What she did remember was a mélange of raised voices in Papa's study, shouts, doors banging, and a pervading feeling of catastrophe.

Bennie—yes, Bennie had been there, as Tom remembered. Bennie seemed part of the family even that long ago. With an effort Althea summoned up recollection. Bennie had been a young lady, just beginning to go to parties. She was staying a month at Darley, being some kind of cousinly relation.

Startlingly, Bennie's white face swam before Althea's mental eye—dark eyes somber and unfocused like a ghost, or like someone who had gone away inside. With a sharp twist of the knife of remembrance, Althea remembered how unnatural it all was, how she had felt that her safe, ordered world was crumbling about her, and there was nothing she could do to save herself.

And finally, at the end of that interminably long day, her own nurse came to tell her that Edward had gone away and she must forget him.

She had thought at the time, of course, that he must have died, but with the self-absorption of the very young she had indeed forgotten him.

Bennie had told her once that Edward had gone to India—and of course, when he had been killed in action near the Khyber Pass—he had attained the rank of colonel in an obscure regiment—the family had been notified.

But none of the story of Edward was real. It was like a tale told, perhaps by Waverley, whoever he was, or even by Lord Byron.

Coming back from memory, she said gently to Tom, "Truly, I don't remember much of him at all."

For once, Tom seemed bereft of words. He muttered something that sounded like, "Wondered, that's all."

He left soon after, refusing coffee—Althea considered that his tongue had been sufficiently loosened not to require a stronger stimulus—but accepting an invitation for Caroline and himself to dinner.

Althea, alone again, was no less uneasy than before. Tom was surely not his usual blustering self, confident that his ideas were the best ideas and his own experiences of absorbing interest to everyone. Caroline's apparent withdrawal from the favors of the marriage bed was in all likelihood making him testy. If he were to divert himself elsewhere, Althea thought, admiring her own broad-mindedness, she for one would not blame him.

With a shock, the obvious parallel smote her. Tom and Simon, and the question of finding satisfaction elsewhere than at home. Simon had point-blank refused to remove that Cyprian from his life. So Althea had removed herself.

But that was different, Althea told herself. Tom and Caroline had never petended to be passionately in love, whereas she and Simon . . . But it must have been pretense, after all. Simon had recovered, so it seemed, and she certainly had.

It was only for the sake of Bennie's health that she was planning to avoid London in the next months. Simon and his plans for marriage had nothing whatever to do with it.

She needed to talk to Bennie. She had not seen her yet this morning, to see for herself the state of her friend's health. Besides, she wanted to tell her that Tom and Caroline were in town and would join them for dinner.

Speaking a word of apology to Tyson for doubting him, she hurried up the stairs to Bennie.

She found her looking much better. "You even have some color in your cheeks," Althea told her, "unless your Kate has applied something out of the pot?"

"No," smiled Bennie, "she did not even soak a red ribbon for the dye in it." She was dressed in a round gown of a drab color, but she wore a Kashmiri shawl of many rich hues around her shoulders. "I am feeling better. Soon I shall be ready to travel to London."

"That's what I wanted to talk to you about, my dear," said Althea. "I am persuaded that London might not be the thing. You must avoid any chance of taking a relapse."

Bennie, mindful of the rumors in the baths, rumors she had passed on to Althea the night before, looked searchingly into Althea's face, and then decided to hold her tongue. Nothing would be gained by thrashing over speculations about Simon's intentions and his future plans. Sleeping dogs, she considered, must be allowed to continue napping.

"Here's something for you to look forward to," said Althea, more gaily than she felt, "after the treatment. Tom and Caroline are in town, and they'll be here to dinner. That reminds me, I must speak to Cook about what to serve. I think perhaps that squabs, in a wine sauce, might do. Caroline certainly must not expect cooking from Mrs. Tyson on the same order as her own French chef." In a thoughtful voice, she continued, "I have heard that if one is required to eat inferior food, one cannot be happy. Would you not think, then, that the contrary would apply? And if one had a French chef, should not one be happy as larks all day long?"

Bennie smiled in appreciation. "Althea, you have such odd humors. I own that Mrs. Tyson's cooking is plain, but certainly well prepared and ample in quantity."

"And," Althea finished for her, "anything more is simply affectation."

"I did not say so," objected Bennie mildly.

"No, but I have not known you all these years for naught!"

Before she left, she brought up the subject that Tom had mentioned. "Tom asked what I remembered about Edward."

The color in Bennie's cheeks receded, providing proof, if needed, that she had spoken truly: there was nothing artificial about her flush.

"Edward? Wh-why?"

"I do not know. He simply asked what I remembered. I told him it was too long ago. But why should he ask? Edward is dead, and he was dead to all of us long before that."

"Not quite all of us," Bennie said, surprisingly. "You know he wrote to me for a couple of years after he left Darley Hall."

"Two years!"

"At least, for a while. And suddenly he didn't write again."

Later Althea thought, A day of shocks! The presence of Tom and Caroline in town and the rift between them, Tom's asking about Edward, and of all things, Bennie's confession that she and Edward had corresponded for a time. Althea was sure that Papa never knew that, or Bennie would have vanished from the household at Darley. Nor, most likely, was Tom aware that Bennie knew Edward better than any of them had suspected.

Things are not what they appear to be, she thought, and shapes moved darkly under the calmest surface. But at least the expedition to the Pump Room, on which they were embarking in a quarter of an hour, would be ordinary.

3

The journey to and from the Pump Room turned out to be uneventful enough. Althea, as always, sent an admiring glance at the abbey just before following Bennie inside.

Sir Horace had come, as was his habit, to escort the ladies for Bennie's treatment. The course of mineral waters suggested by the physician in residence was nearly over. At first Althea had had little faith in the efficacy of the treatment, for three weeks had passed without the slightest improvement in Bennie's health.

But now, the last few days had seen a decided change for the better, and Althea's spirits rose accordingly.

Sir Horace had been faithful in his attendance on the ladies. He was at hand in Laura Place to help Bennie into the carriage, covering her with a multitude of rugs against a possible chill and giving her his arm as they crossed the short pavement before the doors of the Pump Room.

It would have been difficult for an onlooker to judge, simply by watching his demeanor, which of the ladies held the larger share of his interest. Certainly he was attentive to the invalid, but when Bennie had received her two glasses of pungently aromatic mineral waters and lapsed into a restful nap, he offered his arm to Althea and then strolled around the Upper and Lower Rooms, greeting their many friends and acquaintances.

On this day, they moved in silence for a bit. Finally, Sir Horace said, "She is much better, is she not?" Neither had any doubt as to whom he meant.

"Oh, I think so, and I am so relieved. I confess I did not hold out much hope when days went by and I could see no improvement. In truth, it did seem to me she was failing. But now she seems definitely on the mend."

"And you will move on to London soon?"

Some quality in his voice struck her and she glanced swiftly upward at his face. But all she said was, "I do not think so."

When he expressed interest, she continued, "I fear that London will be too strenuous for her, at least for a while. I am thinking more particularly of staying in Bath for much of the spring and summer, and then, before cold weather strikes us, traveling to Italy for the winter."

"Shall you go alone?" He frowned. "Should you not have an escort? Two ladies traveling such a distance, one an invalid—"

"I had not reached that detail," she confessed. "It has been in my mind only since yesterday."

"I see. I agree—Italy may be the proper move." His sidelong glance was full of an understanding that, far from comforting her, was mortifying. She could see as though it were written on his forehead the conviction that the current rumor about Simon and Miss Morton had somehow reached her ears, and she was taking steps to escape confrontation, like the veriest coward alive.

She knew her cheeks were mantled with a rosy flush, but she could do nothing about it. Not only did Sir Horace accurately assess the interpretation that would undoubtedly be placed on her avoidance of London, but also she *was* avoiding Simon, and that in itself was significant. Why would she avoid him, if she were not still nursing a *tendre* for him?

She stifled a strong wish to leave Sir Horace standing where he was in the middle of the Upper Room and finding a bolt hole somewhere.

Instead, she continued walking, smiling and nodding at people she knew, and hoping she would not be called upon to speak until she was sure her voice was under better control. She was fortunate. Lord and Lady Hatton halted their progress.

"Miss Rackham, you sly puss," cried Lady Hatton. "You did not tell us yesterday that Lord and Lady Darley were expected. I was much surprised, I can assure you, when I saw the curtains of the house across the square were opened to the light this morning. The house has been for let for a fortnight, since old Lord Vaubien went home—much better, so I am informed, and we may all rejoice at that. Such a fine gentleman of the old school, you know."

Since Lord Vaubien had been one of the famous habitues of Mendenham, Lady Hatton's description of him seemed sadly awry.

"How did you know that my brother had taken the house?"

"I sent a footman across to inquire," she said without blushing. "He was informed that Lord and Lady Darley had arrived late last evening."

And were you also informed that Caroline is tired of breeding and wishes no more to do with Tom for the present? Suddenly Althea was struck with dread lest she had spoken aloud. But the conversation was going smoothly along, and apparently she had not uttered a sound. But with her thoughts in such tumult, she believed it would be best if she were to remove herself from any possible ill chance.

Removing her hand from Sir Horace's arm, she nodded at the Hattons, murmuring an excuse, and moved on. She passed several chairs, occupied seemingly by oddly assorted bundles of clothing and rugs. If there were humans within the bundles, they were not readily visible.

Only one face could be seen on the patient in the last

chair of this particular rank. The face—female—was of that peculiar sallowness that indicates a sojourn in a tropical country. The eyes were open, and caught Althea's in a mute appeal. She moved to sit beside the invalid. "How are you feeling?"

"Perfectly terrible." The voice, though breathy and weak, held amusement, which must be termed, under the circumstances, gallant.

"I'm so sorry," said Althea, warmly.

"I know you, my dear. Pray do not think me so unmannerly as to solicit perfect strangers."

"Please do not explain," said Althea, worried. The woman appeared to be barely alive. Althea took her hand and held it, trying to lend her some of her own health.

"I knew your mother. May I call you Althea?"

"Of course. But should you not save your strength?"

The eyes closed. Althea wondered how she could extricate her hand from the other's bony clutch. She need not have worried. The lady's maid appeared, looking without favor on her mistress's visitor. "Lady St. Aubyn is tiring, miss."

Lady St. Aubyn! Althea knew that name, although she had never met her. A friend of her mother's, of course, one who had spent most of her married life in India.

Fingers tightened on Althea's and the old eyes opened wearily. "I shall be better soon. My dear, accept my sympathy—on your loss."

The eyes closed then and did not open. A few steps away, Althea questioned the maid. "Lady St. Aubyn is just back from India? Is she—is she very ill?"

"Ill enough, miss." The maid's attitude toward Althea was relaxed now. "But she'll do, all right. Going up to London, she says. I don't think. But she's a big house there, and maybe she'll be all right. But not into society, no, ma'am."

When Althea again joined Sir Horace and they turned toward the chair where they had left Bennie to rest, she did not tell him about meeting Lady St. Aubyn. It was a surprising encounter, meeting someone she had only heard of, in the flesh, and not much of that. But it was the lady's final words that troubled her. Sympathy . . . on her loss. Could she mean the distant relative whose generous legacy had brought independence to Althea? Or even Edward, gone less than two years but still a loss that the family had made little of, not even going into mourning.

Lady St. Aubyn was very ill, Althea reflected, and she could have meant, in her weakness, anything . . . or nothing. She dismissed the encounter from her mind.

"You know, Sir Horace, that Tom and Caroline have arrived in Bath? They are coming to dinner tonight and I should be pleased if you would come too."

"Tom? What's he doing here? He's as healthy as a horse! Oh, I see, it is likely Lady Darley. I trust it is not serious. But, my dear, much as I enjoy dining with you, I think this must be a dinner *en famille*, at least their first night in Bath."

With Sir Horace's assistance, Althea and Bennie were returned to Laura Place, and Bennie settled for a cup of restorative tea before making the ascent to her room to rest for dinner.

"I am so much better," she said, setting the empty cup down. "I declare the waters are miraculous in their curative powers. Or else," she said with a rueful laugh, "the fever ran its course quite naturally. I suspect the latter, and I can tell you the next time I shall not let a drop of that most vile draft pass my lips." She thought for a moment, and added, "I think, dear Althea, that I shall not drink any more Bath water at present, either —I can still taste it."

After Bennie had been helped upstairs to rest, Althea remained in the parlor, watching the sinking fire. She was too lazy to ring for Samuel to build it up. Time enough to make the blaze before Tom and Caroline came. Nor did she want the lamps lit now. For the first time since she had arrived in Bath, she was impatient with her surroundings. The house was poky and narrow, the Pump Room was crowded with malingerers—except, of course, for Lady St. Aubyn, who was truly ill, and probably others in her condition —and one saw the same people over and over again.

The society in which Althea moved was of necessity a limited one. Only a few had the funds to enjoy idleness on a grand scale. Of course, persons engaged in commerce, many of them, were wealthy as nabobs. But for the most part they kept their place, which was not in the exclusive West End of London. Or even here in Bath! If a cit became ill, of course he could undertake a course of treatment. But his presence would be ignored by the Quality as though he did not exist.

Althea drew no conclusions from her musing, save for the dark suspicion that such malaise as engulfed her might well be the harbinger of a megrim at the very least. Resolutely she set her mind against such an infirmity. I don't have time, she told herself crossly. But when she began to make a mental list of things to be done at once, she could think of none.

Amid this state of mind disaster arrived in the form of Miss Jenny Burrell. She followed hard on the heels of Tyson, taking no risk of being denied. Miss Jenny suspected occasionally that she was not as welcomed as she thought. Being capable of enormous self-deception, however, she laid her doubts on the doorstep of a mythical attack of dyspepsia and continued on her malicious way.

"Sitting here in the dark, Miss Rackham?" Miss Jenny cried gaily. "One hopes that is not a sign of guilty conscience, mustn't one? Though what we spinsters could have on our consciences, I could not say."

Althea was instantly angry at the coupling of herself and Miss Jenny in an epithet she despised, especially since it was literally true. We spinsters, indeed!

"May I offer you some refreshment?" Even inner disgust could not erase her impeccable training.

"No, thank you. Well, perhaps a small glass of sherry?"

Upon being furnished with her requirement, Miss Jenny proceeded to the point of her visit. "We live in such a backwater here in Bath, do we not? It is just as though the real world is passing us by, while we know nothing of it. How different it would be if we were domiciled in London. As we soon shall be. I believe the Season is already advanced. Lord Soames has opened his house, you know. Hanging out for a wife, after all this time. One can hardly credit it." She tittered.

"Lord Soames may do as he pleases." Too late, Althea realized her tone had been, to put it kindly, somewhat waspish. She became aware of Miss Jenny's birdlike eyes regarding her brightly, as though she were a particularly promising worm.

"I am so glad to hear that," Miss Jenny resumed when she was sure that Althea intended to say no more. "I did wonder just a bit when I heard the news, but then I said you would rather be *au courant* before you arrived in London. To prepare yourself for the ordeal, you know."

Althea thought she must have missed some vital word of her visitor's. "Wh-what news?" she said faintly.

Miss Jenny looked longingly into her empty sherry glass, but Althea made no move toward the bell. Resigned, Miss Jenny leaned forward and said in a portentous manner, "Lord Soames has offered for Miss Morton."

Althea heard Miss Jenny from a great distance. In fact, Miss Jenny herself was behaving in a very odd manner, first advancing alarmingly and then, quite unaccountably, receding to a far place.

Simon had actually offered!

With a determined muster of her senses, Althea did not faint. But some moments passed before she could again listen.

"Such a change, isn't it? I had not thought Miss

Morton quite the manner of lady to appeal to him. So different from you! But, of course, your betrothal must have been a monstrous mistake, so soon broken, you know, so perhaps Miss Morton will suit after all.''

She will not! thundered Althea, but not aloud.

"Usually gentlemen choose the same kind of female, one after another. I have noticed this many times. I recall my cousin Howard—Lord Tansley, you know. Three wives, all of the same general appearance. They might have been sisters. My dear mother found them all quite difficult. She could never remember the names, you see. Howard was quite indignant with her, without reason, of course, since it was entirely his fault.''

Althea sat as though drugged, as indeed in a way she was. Miss Jenny's spiteful little voice droned monotonously on in a curiously soporific manner. The news of Simon's betrothal, presented as a fait accompli, had divested her of the most rudimentary sense. To huddle here before her own fire and listen to the steady acid drip of Miss Jenny's malice without protest was far out of character.

Her imagination showed her a quick vision of the morrow: Miss Jenny Burrell the center of an avid throng at the baths, busily shredding Miss Rackham's reputation, "I assure you that she was devastated by the news! Still wearing the willow, of course—''

With an effort, she sat up straight and proceeded, as she should have done long since, to rid her parlor of a most unwelcome guest. Pleasantly, she interrupted Miss Jenny, still in full spate. "I really know nothing about Lord Soames, and it would be most improper for me to comment, except to wish him happy.'' The words stuck in her throat. "I must beg you to excuse me. I am much concerned, you may imagine, for Miss Benbow.''

Rising from necessity with her hostess, the gossip managed one last thrust. "Ah, yes. Sir Horace and Mr. Milburn must share your concern. There is much comment that they are frequent visitors. In fact—"

Thoroughly aroused now, Althea blazed, "In fact, I must take pleasure in the knowledge that our slightest concerns provide entertainment for those of our acquaintance blessed with sufficient leisure to busy themselves in an unwarranted fashion with the affairs of others."

Miss Jenny realized that she had been snubbed. Gathering her shawl around her bent shoulders, she stalked to the door. Althea feared she had made an enemy, but she really could not help herself. Such spite, such unhealthy malice! But she suspected that the gossip would not have moved her so greatly had it not seemed to place Simon out of reach forever.

The moment Caroline Darley entered the house that evening, Althea knew that trouble lay ahead. Her sister-in-law, far from looking exhausted as she claimed, appeared to be in blooming health. From past experience, Althea realized that when Caroline was in spirits, she was well on her way to rearranging affairs in light of what she considered best for all concerned.

It rarely occurred to her to consult the wishes of the beneficiaries of her organizational abilities. On the other hand, those on terms of familiarity with her were often to be seen edging out of sight, to no avail.

Dinner passed pleasantly enough. Not until later, when Tyson brought the coffee tray to the parlor and left, did the atmosphere alter. Caroline took on a purposeful air that Althea recognized with misgiving. In her usual forthright manner, Caroline said, "I must say, Althea, you're taking it well."

Althea's response was noncommittal, but she shot an inquiring glance at her brother. His confidence of the morning came back sharply to her. So Caroline had altered their domestic life to her own advantage, if not to Tom's. What could Althea possibly find to say on *that* head?

Tom, as far as her quick glance showed her, was excessively perturbed, as well he might be. Surely Caroline was not preparing to embark upon a narrative of marital felicity, or the lack of it?

Althea, in swift sympathy for Tom, protested, "I do not think—"

Caroline was unaware of the cause of Althea's embarrassment. "There is nothing to be ashamed of. Besides, we are assured that all is legally quite in order."

Althea gulped. Faintly, she murmured, "You have taken legal advice?" Tom had said nothing about a legal separation.

"Of course," said Caroline, pleased with this evidence of her practical nature. "Did you think we wouldn't? In a matter like this we must make very sure."

Belatedly, Althea began to suspect that more than one subject occupied the conversation. She took a firm grip on herself and, treading carefully, said, "I really don't understand what you are talking about."

Her sister-in-law cast a dark glance at Tom. "I might have known," she said with a sigh that said more eloquently than words could have that she found her husband once more lacking in bare essentials, "that you did not tell Althea. And you called here this morning for that very purpose."

Tom did not respond. Althea rose to his defense. "We had important matters to discuss," she informed Caroline. She did not know what she would say if Caroline demanded to know what they were.

"More important than this news?" Caroline lifted an eyebrow in an exquisite expression of faint scorn. "I do not think so. Simply put, dear Althea, you have a niece."

Althea stared at her in open amazement. "Of course I have. Four of them." Surely Caroline could not be so unmaternal as to forget them? Or at least, three of them?

"Dear Althea, pray do not think me demented. I

assure you I am in perfect control of my faculties. And while I confess that I do not precisely *dote* on my girls, I am persuaded that no one can fault me on their account." She took a deep breath and looked at each of her companions as though daring them to take issue with her. None did. "I mean Edward's daughter."

The sudden stillness that dropped on them was broken only by a gasp from Bennie.

"Edward? Had a daughter?" echoed Althea.

Caroline glanced at Tom, waiting for him to explain. It was clear, however, that he had abandoned the conversation for the moment, leaning forward in his chair and clasping his hands between his knees.

Caroline continued. "Oh, he was married. There is, unfortunately, no doubt of that. As I said, we have taken legal advice."

"Who?" The question was startling, coming in a strangled voice from Bennie, who till now had not uttered a word. "Whom did he marry?"

Suddenly Tom returned in his mind from his wandering. "Woman named Margaret Ainsley. Good-enough family."

Caroline added, "She was related, though somewhat distantly, I fear, to old General Sir Lewis Upham."

"Some sort of companion to Lady Upham. So Dedman says."

Bennie, speaking more to herself than to the others, murmured, "An equivocal position, to be sure. Well-bred, but used as a servant. No wonder she leapt at the chance to marry Edward!"

Tom stared at her. "Edward was a damned fine man! She made a good catch in him!"

"I am quite well aware of that," Bennie said with surprising spirit. "But remember, his family had cast him out, an injustice, to be sure, and one I did not readily forgive them for. Not you, of course, Thomas, nor dear Althea. But that, of course, explains everything. I am so glad to know at last."

Althea was the first to find her voice. "Bennie, I

must tell you that *nothing* is explained." Not quite knowing how to phrase her next question, she hesitated too long.

Caroline, always giving short shrift to tact, turned to Bennie. "How nice that you do understand! I assure you it is more than I do."

Althea had been pursuing her own line of thought. "A daughter, Caroline?"

Brought thus forcibly back to her purpose, she said, "Oh, yes. The daughter. Born in India, of course."

"Eighteen," said Tom in outrage. "She is eighteen years old, and Edward never told us."

"I confess I have had grave doubts about the girl," said his wife. "Out of the blue, so to speak. A girl named Lucy. Who knows anything about her?"

Tom roused at her words, which clearly echoed a previous discussion rather like the dying echoes of guns on a battlefield already won. "She's a Rackham, Caroline, and that is all we need to know."

Later Althea was to recall her brother's remark with some poignancy. Just now, she hurried to pour oil upon troubled waters. "Very interesting indeed, Caroline. I shall enjoy thinking—occasionally—about a faraway niece in India, living among tigers and elephants. Even riding, I suspect, in palanquins, although how one gets into them must remain a mystery. A quite exotic prospect, in truth."

Tom burst out, "Far away? You may well wish it! She's not in India!"

"Not in India? Where, then?"

"On her way home."

Caroline interposed, "He means on her way *here*. To England."

"That's what I said. Do you have to correct everything I say, Caroline? I *said*, on her way home."

Caroline's smile was the epitome of forbearance. "I do not suppose she thinks of England as home."

"She damned well better," spluttered Tom. "She's a Rackham, ain't she?"

Althea, rightly ignoring this exchange as merely the common coin of domesticity, wondered, "Why? I mean, why is she coming here? Is her mother sending her to school, perhaps?"

"No, no. Her mother is dead. I do not quite know the details, but the child is an orphan."

Well, thought Althea, it was all too bad, but in truth Edward had vanished from her ken so long before that even now, in this unprecedented family discussion of his affairs, he seemed to have no substance. Like a traditional family ghost, she decided, everyone was aware of its existence, but did not really expect to traffic with it.

Yet, there seemed to be an unfinished air about this entire conversation, a suggestion that something more, quite likely of a most unpleasant nature, was still to come. She rushed into incautious speech— better to find out, than to imagine. This judgment, she learned, was not valid.

"Lucy," said Althea, "will find a summer at Darley quite a change, I should imagine."

A small silence ensued. Then Caroline, with the self-assurance appropriate to the daughter of a line of earls, said, "That question does not arise. We cannot have her at Darley."

Remembering the thirty bedrooms at Darley Hall, as well as nearly a hundred servants, Althea asked on a mystified note, "Why ever not?"

"It should be obvious. She must be introduced into society."

"Introduced?"

"After," Caroline explained, "sufficient instruction."

Helpless in the face of Lady Darley's formidable advance across rough terrain, Althea could only repeat, "Instruction?"

"Pray do not repeat everything I say," admonished Caroline. "It is a most irritating habit. Instructions, of course. You must get the child's colonial habits rubbed off, first. The mother seems to have been passable as to breeding, but the girl is, as my husband says so tediously often, a Rackham." Her tone of voice suggested that this fact was of questionable value.

"Instructed in decorum," mused Bennie.

"And dressed. And sponsored," confirmed Caroline.

Althea, recovering swiftly, demanded, "Why not you? After all, Tom is the head of the family. It is a responsibility I should expect him to be unwilling to delegate. With your background, you are preeminently the proper person—"

Caroline interrupted ruthlessly. "My dear, it is a matter of the simplest nature. I am fully occupied— with my children and my charities." In the manner of one who strikes a final, telling blow, she added, "And you have nothing else to do."

This was quite beyond everything! Althea's anger arrived full-blown. How dared Caroline take over the direction of her life without so much as a by-your-leave! I have plenty to do, she raged inwardly, and in any case, I am not here simply to do the things you don't want to do.

Telling phrases, full of irony, loaded with indignation and protest, swarmed through Althea's mind. An urgent diversion appeared in the form of a memory— "Your overbearing, pompous family, always using you, and you are fool enough to dote on them!" The words had stung, especially since the voice was Simon's in that last far-ranging quarrel. Forced to pause while she considered anew the truth of his accusation, she lost the initiative.

Bennie cried in pleasure, "How wonderful!"

Althea sent a riveting glance of warning in her direction. It was of no avail. "Dear Althea," Bennie continued, "I shall so enjoy doing this. After all, Edward's daughter!" She realized suddenly that three pairs of eyes were fixed on her, in varying degrees of astonishment. She blushed, but continued doggedly, "A most rewarding prospect!"

Confronted by Bennie's shining smile in her too-thin face and the very real delight Althea saw in her eyes, she had no choice but to accede to Caroline's scheme. Undoubtedly her own peace of mind would be destroyed forever. She thought bleakly of Simon's betrothal and wedding to Isobel Morton, in all likelihood taking place directly in front of her eyes. But she owed an enormous debt to Bennie—her support, encouragement, and love over many years.

"Very well," she said, summoning what enthusiasm she could find. "Instruct Mr. Dedman that Lucy is to come to us in Grosvenor Square when she arrives."

How wonderful, indeed!

4

Under the spur of the new project, which Bennie had adopted as primarily her own, her health improved daily and visibly. Since Mr. Dedman, Lord Darley's man of affairs, was informed that Miss Lucy Rackham had booked passage on the *Castle Cliff* out of Bombay, and it was reliably reported that a period of storms had struck the Indian Ocean, there was no great haste in removing from Bath to London.

Bennie's refusal to take another draft of what she termed "the most noxious brew in the world," had caused no relapse in her condition. In fact, she was in a fair way to becoming her old self within the month.

March blew itself out and April danced gently in, and Althea knew it was time to open the house in Grosvenor Square and set out for town. She had found that memories held her in thrall for the moment. It was as well that her thoughts were thoroughly occupied, since Bennie's, volubly expressed, ran solely along the lines of clothing the young Lucy, speculation about her present whereabouts on the dangerous seas, and plans for furnishing a bedroom quite to her liking.

"My dear," Bennie said one morning, "I fear I am taking too much upon myself. If you think it very forward in me, pray tell me so, for I do not mean to be."

"Not in the least."

"It is only that she is Edward's daughter, you

know." Then, apparently feeling that a fuller explanation was expected, she obliged. "Did you know that
Edward and I were betrothed once? No, I see you
didn't. No one else knew, and probably it would have
come to nothing in the end, for my papa had a low
opinion of Edward."

"But he went away!"

"Y-yes. He did. I would have followed him, anywhere. But he did not ask me to." Bennie looked
fixedly at the muffin she was buttering. "I never
believed what they said he did, you know. To think he
could even have fired his pistols at that draper! To say
nothing of wounding him sorely. Ridiculous! I knew
Edward, you see, and he was not at all interested in the
man's daughter. After all, he loved me," she finished in
simple pride.

There was nothing to say. Althea might suspect that
Bennie, prejudiced as she undoubtedly was, had bent
the truth to fit her wish, but there was no reason to
divest her now of opinions that comforted her.

"Why should he not love you?" she said in a lighter
note. "I surely do, and sometimes I suspect Sir Horace
of a strong regard for you." To her delight, Bennie
flushed scarlet, and when she spoke next, it was on
another subject.

The first days in London went swiftly by. Lucy
Rackham progressed toward Grosvenor Square,
Bennie's plans for the girl's welcome sped up, and
Althea found herself at loose ends. Rightly judging
that sooner or later she must face her acquaintance—
all atitter as they must be at the prospect of a confrontation that must be vexations to her in the
extreme. The sooner this meeting, which must be
inevitable, took place, the sooner she would regain her
composure.

On the Wednesday following their arrival from Bath,
with Sir Horace Wychley as her escort, she set out for
Almack's, determined to get the awkwardness of her

first meeting with Simon in two years over and done with. She could not have told whether she longed to see him again, or whether she wished with all her heart that he had not chosen this particular time, when she was constrained by family obligations to move freely in society, to come to London to seek a wife.

Sir Horace's carriage turned into King Street, and the lights of Almack's Assembly Rooms streamed out onto the pavement. They were not too late, she saw, because a couple of carriages drew up to the curb ahead of them, and their occupants, clutching furs against the night dampness, scurried across the walk and up the steps.

The moment Althea entered the Assembly Rooms, she was aware of an aura of quivering expectancy greeting her. Socially fine-tuned, she could judge to a nicety the temper of an occupied drawing room. Just now, noting the quick glances thrown her way, and the even quicker averting of a hundred pairs of eyes, as though she had somehow gone invisible, she was convinced that, at the very least, Isobel Morton, the rumored fiancee—if not Simon himself—awaited her in the inner rooms.

She surrendered her cloak to the hovering maid and stepped forward, Sir Horace a few steps behind her, to greet the hostesses with aplomb.

The Countess of Jersey held Althea's hand a moment too long. The short fingers pressed Althea's significantly. "My dear," she said, "I am delighted that you have returned to us. Your dear Bennie is recovered, I trust?"

Althea murmured a response to Lady Jersey's question. "Much better, thank you, but I insisted she stay at home for a few days longer. The night air, you know—"

The countess had not waited for an answer. Her darting glance fell on Althea's escort. "And Sir Horace, too. Mr. Milburn is still in Bath? I vow it is becoming quite usual to see dear Mr. Milburn in your train." As though suddenly hearing the indiscretions that fell unrestrained from her lips, she gave a laugh that in someone less handsome and less formidable might be deemed a titter.

Althea, a little above the average height, looked over the shoulder of her hostess, searching the room beyond for the face she longed, and dreaded, to see. How would he look? Would he be much altered? A little gray in his tawny hair? Some trace of suffering?

She noted with a sinking feeling all eyes turned toward the door, all faces watching her, waiting for her reaction. And then she saw him.

There was no mistaking Simon Halleck, Lord Soames. Even before her eyes sent her the message of recognition, something squeezed her heart and stopped her breath. In spite of previous rehearsals of her proper response to the first sight of the man she had once loved passionately, she was no better prepared than if he had this minute dropped from the moon.

A part of her mind feared she would blush, but there was no danger of that. Instead, the color drained perceptibly from her cheeks, leaving only circles of rouge standing out.

His appearance was astonishingly familiar. It was as though she had carried the picture of him in her mind, unknowing, all these years, and now he slid into it—as though a two-dimensional portrait had taken on a third dimension.

The mane of tawny hair that swept back from his strong face, the deceptively lazy look in his eyes as he, suddenly aware of the hush that fell over the assembly, turned to seek out the cause, were heart-stoppingly familiar. She knew the precise moment he caught sight of her—his movement arrested; his features, those once dear, familiar features, frozen. His gaze locked with hers. Even from here she knew the precise color of those eyes, more amber than brown, slightly tilted at the outer corners. That calm, penetrating look . . .

Suddenly she could breathe again. Her training, put

to the test, proved to have been superb. Now she spoke again to Lady Jersey, entirely forgot Sir Horace, and moved into the crowd.

She noted, from the corner of her eye, that Lady Lieven, a born mischief-maker, fixed her glittering eyes greedily upon Althea's face, to garner even the least look of dismay. If none was forthcoming, she could easily invent what was needed to create a sensation.

Althea's lip lifted in contempt, but she held her tongue. What she might have said or done, she would never know, for the violins struck up for the next dance and animation returned to the assembly at Almack's.

The room was so well known to her that she could have itemized the furnishings in her sleep: the balcony at the far end for the musicians, the massive chandeliers, the draped Greek notable in a niche along the wall. She saw nothing of it now. It was strangely as though she and Simon were completely alone in the room.

Simon spoke briefly to his companions, among whom she recognized black-haired Isobel Morton in a gown that was so in the forefront of fashion that the seamstress must have finished it that very day. He moved unhurriedly, in the smooth glide she knew so well, through the couples moving onto the dance floor. He reached her, took the hand she offered him as a sleepwalker might, and bowed over it. He led her unresisting onto the dance floor.

She was vaguely aware that the musicians played from the balcony, other couples swirled around her, and her feet in their heelless satin slippers moved in the fast steps of the waltz. Surely she was mistaken—no one truly moved six inches above the floor?

When she at last was able to look up at him, letting her steps mind themselves in the dance, she gasped inwardly. His demeanor was excessively correct, but his eyes told her another story.

Her breath caught in her throat. Could he be—he

could *not* be angry with her still, not after this long time.

"I am told," he said presently, "that you have been at Bath. I trust your health is now restored?"

"I have not been ill."

"Indeed. You do appear to be in excellent looks."

"I am."

They waltzed in silence. Then, fearing she had been uncivil in her short reply, she resumed, "And you?"

His thoughts must have turned into new channels, for he looked absently at her. "I beg your pardon," he said.

"You were not listening," she agreed. "A failing of yours about which I have had occasion to speak before."

"Indeed you did. And you spoke very well too." The words may have been innocuous, but the tone in which they were uttered was quite otherwise. "If at tedious length!"

Althea was recovering from the ordeal of seeing him again. Indeed, she considered, it was as though the years apart had vanished. But there was still too much lying between them, too many accusations, too much bitterness, to resume where they had left off. In fact, they had terminated their betrothal in the furnace of an anger that, she realized, had barely had sufficient time to cool.

Impelled by lack of courage, however, to speak of essentials, she resorted to mere civility. "The country must be lovely this time of year."

"And yet you have not visited Darley Hall since you removed to London. Two years and three months ago."

"How do you know?"

He clearly wished the words unspoken again. But he said only, "My sister keeps me informed."

Althea, in a falsely cordial tone, responded, "Emma. Of course she does. Lady Fabyan has always held your interests above her own."

Simon ignored the thrust. "Is your avoidance of

Darley Hall an avoidance—entirely understandable—of the company of your relation?"

Althea remembered vividly that her intense devotion to her brother and his brood had figured prominently in the famous quarrel. "Not at all," she said sweetly. "In truth, I dote on them."

He smiled grimly. "I can always discern a falsehood on your lips." The word "lips" appeared to unsettle him momentarily. Recovering, he changed the conversation. "I too have a family to consider. I am in London out of duty to them."

"Duty?"

"To seek a wife, of course. The line must continue." He added, "Dear me, I must have stepped on your toe. My apology."

"Not at all," she said stiffly, never in the world admitting that his bald statement had caused her to miss a step.

They had traversed one side of the ballroom before, with a wicked gleam in his amber eyes, he said, "Perhaps you can recommend someone to me? I require a docile young lady, of excellent family, it goes without saying. One who will preside over my house with competence and calmness."

Irritated, Althea snapped, "Qualities you may find in a nursery governess."

"I have no wish to seem indelicate, but of course a nursery must come under her supervision. Duty to the family must be her purpose, of course." Apologetically, he continued, "Dear me. How flushed you are! Perhaps it is the heat in the room, although I myself find it quite cool."

He was infuriating! He knew her entirely too well, he knew the weak spots in her armor, and he had no compunction about probing them—with a sharp pointed word. She could cheerfully strangle him. Not in public, of course. Somewhere very private.

He went too far. "May I solicit your assistance in my

quest?" If he expected her to express a willingness to return instead to his arms, he was disappointed.

"Indeed you may," she said with spirit. "I suggest someone of intelligence, to preside, you know, over the education of your children, for I am persuaded you have not the least notion of how to go on."

He looked at her in surprise. The waltz was drawing to a close, and he searched frantically for a word to keep her in conversation with him.

She was entirely willing to keep in his company, at least until she had said what she intended to convey to him. "Miss Morton is a notable bluestocking. But of course you know that. I am persuaded you have already made your offer, so there is very little advice for me to give you."

"Miss Morton!"

The dismayed expression on the once-loved features gave her the liveliest satisfaction.

"I am sure you will find in her, perhaps not all that you desire, but certainly all that you deserve."

He was truly angry now. As he escorted her back to Sir Horace, she could feel the muscles of his forearm rigid under her fingertips. Before they reached Sir Horace, he said in a voice low enough not to carry, "At least she would be docile, a quality I cannot sufficiently praise."

The rest of the evening was lost to her. Her own thoughts tumbled and turned. Seeing Simon had been sufficient to overset her. But his conversation was of a nature to infuriate her.

She was angry at his assumption that she was interested in his affair, to the point of asking her advice! He had never taken it before, when she had a claim upon him, and she could not prevent herself from realizing that his request was a clear indication that she was no longer part of his plans.

Docile, indeed!

She would never qualify, never in the world. She

was totally lacking in that characteristic. But the worst of it was, she recognized in herself a very strong feeling that, whatever Simon said or did, she could never treat him with indifference.

And, with a sinking conviction that she could not easily let him go, she thought, If he wants docile, I can give him docile!

It did not cross her mind to wonder what would happen when her supply of demure docility, grafted as it must be onto a substantially more unruly disposition, was expended.

5

At last the evening was over. She was enormously grateful to Sir Horace for discerning her mood and preserving silence on the drive to Grosvenor Square. On the other hand, possibly his thoughts rested comfortably on Bennie, and Althea was forgotten.

She closed her eyes to ease her throbbing head and opened them only when Sir Horace's carriage slowed for the turn into Brook Street. All she wanted now was the ministrations of Pinkham, too drowsy to talk, and a hot brick in her bed.

Her wishes were not fulfilled. Tyson opened the door promptly upon the sound of carriage wheels, with an expression of excitement barely concealed on his face. She could hear voices from the drawing room. She bade Sir Horace good night and, as soon as the door closed on his heels, turned to her butler.

"What is amiss, Tyson? Miss Benbow is not worse? No, she can't be, for I fancy I hear her voice."

"Lord Darley arrived earlier this evening, miss. He did not wish word to be sent to you, preferring to await your return."

"Tom! Here? At this hour?"

She hurried into the drawing room, untying the ribbons of her cloak as she went. Tyson hurried after her, preventing the garment from falling to the floor in her wake.

Her drawing room was furnished in muted blue, of

the particular shade fancied by Josiah Wedgwood, enlivened with gold. A pair of gold brocade chairs faced each other near the fireplace, and in them sat her brother Tom and Bennie. It was, thought Althea suddenly, a calm room. Since she had furnished it herself, perhaps she could detect an omen here? She must have docility somewhere in her, else she could not admire such a room.

"There you are," boomed Tom, rising. He always spoke as though he were following the hounds—in fact, following far behind the pack. He looked closely at her. "These late nights don't do you any good, you know. Lose your looks, and then who'll have you?"

"Pray, Tom, don't ring any peals over me tonight. I trust that Caroline is well, and the children?"

"Caroline's not quite the thing. This whole business of Lucy troubles her, you know."

But not, thought Althea, sufficiently to lead her to stir herself on the girl's behalf.

Bennie rose. "My dear, I'll leave you two. I'll just tell Pinkham to bring you a posset at bedtime, Althea, to help you sleep. I suspect your headache has returned? You do look quite pale."

"I shall be glad of my bed. Do you go along, Bennie, and sleep late. You should not have stayed up for me."

"I merely kept Lord Darley company," Bennie said. She smiled at them, and left.

After the door was closed quietly behind her, Althea said, "Now, Tom, I gather that you have already warned the servants that you are staying overnight."

"I believe Bennie did."

He took up a small snuffbox from the table and looked at it as though he had not seen it before, even though it had been in the family for two generations.

"I hear Soames is in town."

"News travels fast."

"Wonder what he wants. Hanging out after you again?"

"What nonsense!" She felt her cheeks warming.

"Everyone will say—well, dammit, looks like you can't wait to see the rogue again," grumbled her brother. "All I can say is I hope you won't take him back after the shabby treatment he dealt you."

"If that is truly all you have to say, and I hope devoutly it is, I assure you that Lord Soames means nothing to me anymore."

With one of the unexpected flashes of shrewdness that visited Lord Darley at irregular intervals, he glanced at her. "I suppose your headache has nothing to do with the man? Did he ask to call on you? I shall hope to have something to say to that."

"Tom, dear Tom," she begged, "pray do not vex me tonight. If you came to town to protect me from Simon, I assure you there is no need." Nor any use, she added silently. The great Lord Soames is looking for a docile wife. I could never suit him.

"Not Soames. I can deal with him!"

"What is amiss, then?" She sighed, without even attempting to conceal her weariness. "Don't try to bam me, Tom. You have something on your mind. I know the signs." When he did not answer at once, she added, "For goodness' sake, tell me at once. You've lost your fortune? You've come to tell me Darley Hall has been swept away in a windstorm? Do tell me why you've come up to town, Tom, so I can go to bed."

"Ever hear of a feller name of Cosgrove?"

"Cosgrove?" She consulted memory. "No. Who is he?"

"I'll be damned if I know. Dedman's got me up to town. Meeting tomorrow. Here."

"Here? In my house? Tom, if you're going to conduct your business in town, I strongly suggest that you open up your own house."

"No reason to," he answered. "You've got enough spare rooms for all the family."

Althea had had a long day. The encounter with Simon would have been sufficient to send another woman fainting with exhaustion to her bed. It was no

wonder that she allowed exasperation to be heard
in her voice. "I really cannot countenance this, Tom.
Why does not Mr. Dedman ask you to his office? Or
better yet, come down to Darley Hall, as he has done
many times." A possibility struck her unpleasantly.
"Your meeting, I suppose, does have to do with your
affairs, and not mine?"

"He didn't tell me."

"I should not think he would send for you, in that
event, when he knows I am in town. Unless . . ." she
mused, pursuing her own line of thought. "Tom, do
you suppose Lucy's ship has gone down?"

He was startled. "Heard something, have you?
You're always the first to hear all the gossip, I suppose
because you have nothing else to do but to listen."

"I'm listening to you, Tom. I have heard nothing
about a ship sinking."

The silence between them lengthened. Finally, she
rose briskly. "I suppose Bennie has put you in your
usual room," she said in a practical tone of voice
designed to signal an end to the evening. "I do hope
you have not come all the way to London simply to
give me your support against Simon. But it was dear of
you to come."

"Got to meet this Cosgrove feller tomorrow. Told
you that."

"I regard that as fustian. Whoever he is, Tom, he
should have gone to you at Darley Hall."

It did seem to her, however, that Tom was truly
uneasy in his mind on the subject of Mr. Dedman, Mr.
Cosgrove, and the approaching interview. Nonetheless, no matter if the sky fell in, she would not consider
anything more this night. She stood on tiptoe and
kissed his cheek. "Ask Tyson for anything you need.
Good night, Tom."

Althea was driving in the park the next afternoon at
the hour fixed for the visit of Mr. Dedman and Mr. Cosgrove. Her curiosity had run riot all morning, but since

Tom knew no more than she did, there was little to learn from him. He had the impression that the interview had something to do with the approaching arrival of Miss Lucy Rackham, and wished Althea to remain within call.

"Certainly not," she told him firmly. "You and Caroline have wished the girl on me. While I do not object to the prospect, particularly since Bennie has come nobly to my assistance"—in truth, Bennie was arranging the whole—"I would have been much more in charity with you both had you seen fit to discuss it with me first. But to the idea of allowing Mr. Dedman to prose on to me about an affair which is in the last resort your responsibility—no, thank you, Tom. I shall be home in time to dress for dinner."

The interview was prolonged. It was still in progress when she returned from her drive in late afternoon. Tyson was hovering in the hall.

"The closed door to the drawing room, Tyson. Am I to understand that Mr. Dedman is still with Lord Darley?"

"Yes, miss. Mr. Dedman and a gentleman." Thus neatly docketing the lawyer's place in the scheme of things, he continued, "Lord Darley has asked me to tell you that he expressly desires your attendance immediately upon your return." He coughed to indicate that the words and the summons were none of his.

She made a moue, handed her cloak and bonnet to him, and went into the drawing room.

"Here you are," said Tom, unnecessarily. "We've been waiting."

"Indeed? Mr. Dedman, I hope I see you well?" She offered him her hand.

"May I present Mr. Cosgrove, Althea? My sister."

Mr. Cosgrove bowed stiffly. She regarded him with lively curiosity. Not above the middle height, his stocky build made him seem shorter. His curling hair, a little shorter than the fashion, was sandy, and his thick straight eyebrows only a shade darker. An unprepossessing man, she thought, until she looked into a pair of intensely blue eyes.

"Mr. Cosgrove," explained Tom, "has brought us some news."

Unpalatable, by the look of it, decided Althea. "Indeed? Pray let us be seated, and you may tell me."

"It seems," said Mr. Dedman after the sniff and cough that preceded his every speech, "that Mr. Cosgrove has come to London particularly to be married." The little lawyer's eyes held a momentary spark of amusement at the sight of Althea's surprise.

"I wish you happy," she murmured civilly, wondering why she was made privy to the nuptials of a stranger.

Mr. Cosgrove bowed again. "Thank you, Miss Rackham." A touch of brogue was evident in his speech. From Ireland? She was more mystified than ever.

"Dedman, you take too much time. I'm a busy man, even if you aren't," Tom interrupted. "Long and short of it, Althea, Cosgrove here is set to marry young Lucy! Never heard of such a thing. But there it is! Month ago I never heard of Lucy."

Althea turned to Mr. Cosgrove. She could not say at once that she liked him, but there was a quality of steadiness, even of authority in the way he held himself, that demanded her respect. Especially was his demeanor to be admired when contrasted to the fussy distress exhibited by Mr. Dedman and the overt bewilderment of Lord Darley. She knew she herself must appear somewhat stunned.

"Tell me, Mr. Cosgrove, about my niece. I do not profess to understand what I have just learned, and I am quite prepared to like Lucy—but I am most curious. What is she like?"

Mr. Cosgrove seemed embarrassed. "I do not know, Miss Rackham. I have never met her."

"Never?"

Mr. Dedman intervened. "An equivocal position, yes

indeed, equivocal. A betrothal, you must understand, Miss Rackham, but then again, not precisely a betrothal."

"Then," said Althea with commendable patience, "what is the arrangement?"

Mr. Cosgrove, who had spent a difficult two hours with Mr. Dedman and Lord Darley, realized that he had come upon a receptive audience. He proceeded to inform her. "My father was colonel in a regiment posted to India when I was five years old. He never came home again."

"Like Edward," murmured Althea.

"He became friends with Colonel Rackham, and when Lucy was born, it seemed to them a good idea to form a permanent alliance by contracting Lucy and me for marriage at a suitable time."

"Papers signed—all that!" shouted Lord Darley, giving vent to exasperation. "Tomfool notion!"

"So," said Althea, grasping the kernel of the discussion, "you are indeed betrothed to Lucy? You expect to honor this agreement you had nothing to do with making?"

Mr. Cosgrove shrugged his broad shoulders. She feared for the seams of his new coat, fresh from Weston's workshop. They held.

Suddenly Mr. Dedman became for the moment human. "I do not like these arrangements made in childhood. It is, admittedly, an agreeable situation many times, to be sure that the future is secure, but there is no tampering with the ways of Providence, Miss Rackham," he said, turning sharply to her as though accusing her of attempting to rearrange the universe. "No tampering!"

"But surely, Mr. Cosgrove," Althea inquired, "since the match was apparently been an accepted thing, you will have corresponded?"

He shook his head. He had clearly decided that Althea was the only one of his present companions who was in any way sensible. "One might well think so."

Agitation thickened his voice. "And if her mother had been alive, I must believe our acquaintance must have been duly strengthened in such a way."

"Mother?" said Tom. "What about her mother? Dead, ain't she?"

"Shortly after Lucy's birth, I believe. That was one reason Colonel Rackham was anxious to get his daughter settled."

Althea regarded him with sympathy. "How very hard for you, Mr. Cosgrove. Betrothed all these years to a lady you have not even seen."

"But you see," he explained, "It isn't *real* to me. Always it has been like a tale told by old women sitting by the peat fire in the winter."

Odd, she thought, how his accent becomes more Gaelic when his thoughts turn poetical.

"Some lady far away promised to me," he continued, "and someday she would be my bride. It's been a help, you know, for I did not have to worry about falling into the matrimonial trap. Not that I'm such a fine catch, but I have some fortune and there were times—" He wiped his brow, remembering, it was clear, some of those occasions when he must have been at risk.

Thomas had been fidgeting during this exchange. Mr. Dedman from long experience recognized the preliminary warning indications of imminent eruption. Hastily he gathered his papers.

"Come, Mr. Cosgrove, let us be on our way. There is a letter in my office I must ask you to examine."

Althea doubted the existence of any such letter, but joined heartily in speeding Mr. Dedman and his companion on their way.

After they had left, reaction engulfed her. Can this be true? she wondered wildly, believing that she must have strayed into a world all atilt, where ordinary things turned under one's hand into marvels like the dreams one had after eating crab cakes at midnight. A niece complete with fiance where none was before— surely she had dreamed it all?

"Betrothed?" she said, as if repeating the word would give the idea substance. "Lucy betrothed?" Then, hardly knowing what she said, she added, "That's all right, then."

"What do you mean?" Tom had reached the point of explosion. "Nothing's all right. Don't be so hen-witted! We've got a niece we never heard of—and one I daresay, if she takes after her father, is going to be a handful and a half for you. And now some man I never heard of says he's going to marry her and carry her off to some foreign place, and good riddance, no doubt. But dammit, she's a Rackham and I will not allow such ramshackle goings-on in my family."

"What do you mean to do, then? The marriage has been arranged, the bridegroom is certainly eligible—that is, I assume Mr. Dedman has been to the trouble of investigating the man's antecedents?"

"*And* his worth. Not a nabob, but enough to go on with. Unless I'm greatly mistaken, Edward never had a feather to fly with. The girl will be taken care of."

"Then I see no objection to the marriage, except, of course, her age. You said she was only eighteen? Really, Tom, she may be too colonial to come into society."

"I don't understand any of that," complained Tom. "Women's business, after all. Caroline wants her out and married off. That's all I know."

"Well, then," said Althea, thinking unruly if not downright rebellious thoughts to which she did not give voice, "we have half the battle won." To his inquiring gaze, she answered, "Ninny, Lucy's as good as married already! And you would be greatly misguided if you interfered in any way."

She recalled then one phrase of her brother's that had not seemed pertinent at the time. Now, upon reflection, she wished clarification. "What did you mean, Tom—a handful and a half for me?"

"Why, I mean," he said with suspicious innocence, "with getting her into society and teaching her how to go on. What else would I mean? You agreed to do it."

"And I shall," she told him, allowing irritation to be evident in her voice. "But Caroline must, of course, being the daughter of an earl as she is pleased to remind us at all too frequent intervals, assume the responsibility of Lucy's marriage to Mr. Cosgrove. It is entirely inappropriate for me—"

She realized that Tom's attention was no longer fixed on the matter at hand. Indeed, he was staring at her as though he had received sudden enlightenment on a subject long puzzling him.

"No wonder Soames cried off," he said with fraternal bluntness.

"Cried off?" she shrieked, unable to resist following this red herring dragged across her path.

"Couldn't see marrying a shrew—that's it! You whistled a fortune and a title down the wind. Don't look to me for sympathy." He pondered a moment. "Too late for it, anyway."

Althea sorted through the cutting phrases that came to her lips, but could not choose among them. Shrew, was she? Her whole self rebelled at such an assessment, but somehow each phrase that came to her seemed suddenly to take on an aspect that lent color to her brother's accusation. Finally, seeing Tom's inquiring eye on her, she knew she must respond.

She managed, weakly, "That's all past."

Spurred by a sudden shrewdness, he advised her, "I wouldn't expect him back, you know. That cat won't jump, you may be sure of that."

Stung, she retorted, "You would be better advised to consider what you will do about Edward's daughter."

"I can't expect Caroline to take on getting the girl married off," he confessed at last. "Never liked the idea of Edward in the family. Black sheep, she called him. Black sheep, bad blood. All nonsense, of course, but I had the devil of a time talking her 'round." He thought for a moment. "Made a mistake. Should have let her go. Saw it too late."

Swept by sympathy, she put her hand on his arm. "Caroline really should arrange the wedding. It's her duty." And Lady Darley was always ready to point out duty—particularly that of others.

Tom, once more in charity with his sister, confessed, "I'm not such a flannelhead that I don't know that. But, to tell truth, it's well, it's damned difficult."

"But a wedding without Caroline's sponsorship would give rise to such scandal as I do not wish to contemplate."

"Perhaps—if I point out the scandal . . ."

There was a wealth of emotion in his voice: a simple, uncomplicated man faced with the puzzle of an obstinate woman, a man with inchoate longings that he suspected would remain forever unfulfilled. Althea was moved.

"Of course I'll take the girl now and see that she comes up to the mark. We can discuss her wedding later," she said recklessly. "After all, what trouble can a girl safely betrothed cause?"

In the event, Althea would look back on that moment and marvel at her innocence. At the time, though, she basked in the light of duty done, of generosity displayed and, though she would not have admitted it under torture, in the thought that she now in Lucy had the best of reasons to spend the spring, not in Bath, as she had considered, but in London, where Simon Halleck, Lord Soames, was in residence.

6

Tom, his interview with Mr. Dedman less distressing than he had feared, returned to Darley Hall. In due course, Mr. Dedman, now prepared to deal with Althea in the place of her brother, brought news of the sighting of the four-masted Indiaman *Castle Cliff* off the Downs.

"The hour is at hand, dear Bennie," said Althea, concealing her apprehension under the cover of mock dramatics. "After all, it is not every day one receives into the affectionate bosom of the family a full-grown niece who had not existed, so to speak, a fortnight since."

"At least," Bennie pointed out, "she must have existed, you know, somewhere. Is it not odd to consider that thousands and thousands of people exist somewhere this very moment, and we shall never know?" Bennie's vague smile included in her goodwill all persons of the world, seen or unseen. Such sweetness of disposition was one of the qualities in her companion Althea usually found endearing, but today it was more irritating than comforting.

"I shall never feel their absence," said Althea.

Mr. Dedman planned to escort them to the East India Docks. Althea suspected he would much rather have gone alone, but he was not required to deal with Bennie's excitement and her childlike anticipation of seeing the child of the man she had pledged her love to, twenty years before.

Althea could not refuse Bennie the right to meet the ship. But when Mr. Dedman sent word that pressure of affairs would keep him from accompanying them, she said, "I do hate to see you go down to the docks alone."

"But I shall have John the coachman, and Bell, and a footman to help with the trunks. At least, I suppose there will be trunks."

"All the same, I think I shall go too. I can stay in the carriage if the crowds are rowdy. I believe I must be as curious as you are. I am most impatient to see Edward's daughter, even though I scarcely recall my brother himself."

Their route lay through crowded streets, turning off onto Houndsditch, then to East Smithfield, past the Royal Mint. The area through which they traveled becoming ever more shabby and disreputable in appearance, at last they went along Wapping High Street and East India Dock Road, through the great gates onto the docks.

From that point on, Althea was struck by a mélange of sights, a conglomeration of sounds and smells that ever after swam together in her mind like the unaccountable, constantly shifting images in a dream.

John drove his four as far as he dared along the docks and came to a halt. Bell conferred with him and ran back to tell Althea, "Miss, John say fur as he can go. Have to hoof it"—he blushed fiery red—"begging your pardon, miss. Have to walk from here." With a sweeping gesture, he pointed. "*Castle Cliff* be there."

Althea could make out among all the tangle of masts and rigging what appeared to be the bow of a great ship. She glanced at Bennie, who already had her hand on the door.

"Very well, Bell," said Althea. "Let down the steps for Miss Benbow. You and Samuel will go with her. Don't leave her for an instant!"

Left alone in the carriage with only John on the box, Althea beguiled the time, not in speculating about Lucy, and Mr. Cosgrove, and the alteration her arrival would make—and already made—in the even tenor of life at Grosvenor Square, but in gazing entranced at the bustle around her on the docks.

There had been, and would be, sufficient time to consider all the facets of Lucy's arrival. But in all likelihood Althea would not come this way again. The East India Docks were unique in her experience.

She gave herself up to sheer enjoyment. There were bales and baskets and barrels and wagons as far as the eye could see. She knew that the East India Docks were only part of a huge area of shipping wharves, including the London Docks, St. Katherine Docks, the West India Docks.

The area surrounding her coach was full of people. She did not know the occupations of all of them, but she could recognize clerks, and carters, and customs' men, and swarthy sailors from tropical lands.

Her ears were assaulted by hoarse shouting in many languages, by the heavy rumbling of wagon wheels, the shuddering shrieking of winches. And no curtains could prevent the smells of tobacco, wine, grain, spices, from filling the carriage.

After some time the strange sights and sounds palled and she became restive. Then she caught sight of an unusual eddy in the crowd nearby and strained to see what was at the center.

It was a traveling coach and four, newly arrived on the dock, carrying several servants in livery. The equipage was obviously there to meet someone on the *Castle Cliff.* Her curiosity grew, especially when she recognized the Fabyan crest, as well known to her as the Soames arms. Lady Fabyan was Simon's sister, and Althea recalled all too well the last time she had seen her.

Simon's older sister, and the rest of society, had undoubtedly considered at length the possible causes

of the break between Simon and Althea. To Lady
Fabyan, however, the fault could never lie with Simon,
and she was excessively cool to Althea whenever they
met.

Simon had retreated—not in pique at their broken
engagement, but most likely in high dudgeon—to his
country seat. Althea, though inclined to keep her
upstairs bedroom at Darley Hall and cry for months,
was too proud to go into a decline in public. Her timely
legacy arriving, she had soon removed to London and
was once again seen everywhere, never with the same
escort on more than two consecutive occasions.

Now, Althea, moved by the sight of the Fabyan
crest, was carried back into memory. The sight of
Simon at Almack's the other evening had stirred
emotions she had thought long buried. The recent
erruption of Mr. Cosgrove into her life had occupied
her thoughts for the moment. But Simon was hanging
out for a wife, and all Althea could do was wish him
well.

Unless, of course, she managed to become docile!

Suddenly, even with countless people around her,
she felt the sweep of loneliness engulf her. Was it all to
come down to this, sitting alone in her carriage, comfortable, even cosseted, with an endless round of calls
to make, callers to receive, parties and balls to attend,
to the gossip that spilled over like sewage fouling all
who listened . . . ?

What a gloomy mood! She shook herself and looked
again at her surroundings.

Emerging from the crowd came a figure so startlingly familiar that she gasped. A mane of brownish-
gold hair, a tall well-built figure, some measure of
grace in his walk—it could not be Simon! It was not. It
was his nephew Noel Fabyan. And of course it was for
him that the carriage waited.

Close behind him came Bennie, accompanied by a
slender figure, who must be Lucy Rackham. Althea's
breath stopped in her throat from excitement. The girl

was dressed in a dark-colored gown. Althea recalled Lady St. Aubyn's murmured word of condolence in Bath. Surely the child was out of mourning. Her father had been dead for eighteen months.

The girl looked to be well worth dressing, judging from the grace in her walk. An unworthy thought, Althea told herself, but how should one conduct oneself in such a situation? Nothing her training had informed her of the words, or even thoughts, appropriate to meeting a niece one had never heard of.

The footman opened the door and let the steps down, and Bennie, taking the girl by the arm, said, "And here is your aunt Althea, my dear. Best get into the carriage and we can soon be away from this noisy crowd."

Whatever Bennie was saying to her, Althea did not hear. She was entranced by the vision that stood diffidently before her. Lucy Rackham was, quite simply, the most beautiful girl Althea had ever seen.

Her hair, naturally curling, was black and glossy, caught up by a ribbon of the same violet as her remarkably large and lustrous eyes. Her brows were arched and her complexion like the bloom of a fresh peach. Her mouth was small, with a tendency to pout in a manner that Althea was convinced would drive half the beaux in London quite distracted.

She was well worth dressing!

Bennie touched Lucy's arm. "Give Samuel your handbag. It will be entirely safe with him. Althea, Lucy has no trunks."

Althea glanced sharply at her friend, but Bennie's expression was unreadable. Traveling for months on a sailing vessel with no trunks? Even while she was speaking words of welcome to her niece, Althea felt a prickle of uneasiness, gone before she could discover why. Doubtless, she decided, only the natural apprehensions of the situation itself.

The surprises were not over for the day.

The Fabyan coach had begun to maneuver its way

through the drays, the hacks for hire, the many impediments to easy travel. Suddenly it stopped just ahead of them, preventing their progress. "What a fine carriage," Lucy murmured. "He must be enormously wealthy, but one would not think it to talk with him. He was most kind on the voyage."

Lord Fabyan had left his coach and approached them. With a pleasing combination of boyish friendliness and excellent manners, he addressed Althea. "Good day, Miss Rackham. You may not remember me, but I recall you and Miss Benbow very well."

Seen at close hand, Althea realized Noel Fabyan was but a pale image of Simon, a reflection seen in a dusty glass. Just as well, she sighed inwardly, the world has no room for two Simons.

"You have just come off the *Castle Cliff,* I collect? Have you been traveling extensively?"

"Through the Mediterranean, now that old Bony is out of it. A fine trip, especially the last part of it." He glanced at Lucy. She did not raise her eyes to him, but fixed her gaze demurely on her hands in her lap. "I broke my journey at Funchal."

The Rackham horses moved restlessly, and Noel broke his conversation short. "I shall hope to call soon, to see how Miss Lucy has withstood the voyage." As he spoke to Althea, he could not take his eyes from Lucy. It was only the beginning, she thought, of the wide swath the girl would cut. Mr. Cosgrove would be delighted with her.

Bennie, now seated beside Althea, beamed upon young Noel Fabyan. Quickly sympathetic to his obvious admiration of her charge, she murmured, "It will be pleasant . . ." A glance at Althea stopped her, however, and she let the rest of the sentence trail away.

Althea was indeed struck with the girl's beauty. But she had sufficient experience with her world to know that such looks would give rise to floods of jealousy among the young ladies already in the thick of things. It never hurt to move slowly, at least at first.

Already the girl was creating difficulties, thought Althea, although of course without meaning to. There was Claude Cosgrove of the equivocal betrothal; there was the introduction of the girl to society that Tom mandated; there was the real doubt—judging by the unassuming and even dowdy apparel she wore—that Lucy was ready to move into the tight little society without disaster of one kind or another. First, Althea thought, like a general expecting atttack, she must survey the field.

"I think," she said civilly to Lord Fabyan, "it may not be convenient to receive you for a few days."

Unused to rejection of even a slight nature, Noel flushed darkly under his tanned skin. "I quite understand," he said, obviously not understanding at all. He bowed correctly, if stiffly, and returned to his carriage.

Lucy threw her aunt an infinitely swift glance of extreme dislike, but Althea did not notice. Bennie, however, saw the quick glint in the girl's violet eyes and lapsed into a silence full of unease.

Althea could no longer complain of being bored, of looking forward without enthusiasm to an endless drudgery of days with only frivolity and, if she chose, flirtation to beguile her. Sitting beside her on the velvet cushions of her coach was an unknown quantity in the person of Lucy Rackham. Strangely, the actual presence of this spectacular beauty was curiously oppressive.

In Althea's thoughts, Edward's daughter had moved from the shocking knowledge of her bare existence, through childhood, and swiftly now to adulthood in only a fortnight. If she were eighteen, she was a remarkably ripe eighteen. Of course, everyone said that a life in the tropics caused women to mature more rapidly, and if Althea had just now been introduced to her without previous knowledge, she might easily conclude the girl—the woman—to be in her early twenties. So must Lord Fabyan have judged her.

But still, that untouched dewy freshness of her

beauty was eloquent of extreme youth. If no other satisfaction were forthcoming, at least Althea could look forward to a year of stunning success in society, presenting this great beauty to the world in which she would move. How odd to have a gazetted belle—in potential at least—sitting beside her!

"Lucy was surprised to see me," Bennie said. "In fact, it took me quite some moments before I could convince her of my identity." She laughed ruefully. Clearly, Lucy's doubts of her intentions still troubled Bennie. Of all people, Bennie was the most respectable in appearance of anyone she knew.

"I am sorry," said Lucy with a timid air. "I did not know I was to be met."

As they left the pungent aroma of the docks behind them, they emerged into a London blanketed with mist. The April sun still forced its way through the overhanging heaviness, but it was only a matter of time before the mist thickened into fog, and the city would be separated into small isolated areas.

Fog of a sort had already moved stealthily into Althea's mind. The attitude of Lord Fabyan was equivocal, to say the least. He seemed to be on terms of perfect understanding with Lucy, but only last month had the announcement of his betrothal to Miss More been published.

Bennie too had fallen silent. She could not discover the cause of her uneasiness, but troubled she was. For no matter how English Lucy was by birth, no matter how acceptable her breeding, there was no doubt but that she had been brought up in what was, after all, a heathen land with exotic customs. That quick look Lucy had sent in Althea's direction was nothing in itself, but Bennie could not rid herself of a feeling that it held a significance she could not guess. She decided, with unaccustomed pessimism, that if they all emerged on the far side of the next months with any kind of credit, even without disaster, they would do well.

The thoughts of the young lady, who was the cause of disquiet among her companies, were locked at least for the moment behind that alabaster brow and those spectacular violet eyes.

7

The next fortnight slid swiftly past, one day being much like another. The house seemed overrun with Miss Hope, the little woman who sewed extravagantly beautiful garments for Althea and Bennie and certain other fastidious ladies of fashion, and her assistants who were charged with providing Miss Lucy Rackham with sufficient ball gowns, walking dresses, carriage dresses, a riding habit, and morning dresses to see her safely through the Season just beginning.

A gown, of course, was nothing without the requisite shawls, gloves, bonnets, spencers, kid shoes, and satin slippers of various hues, and even, should occasion warrant, a swansdown muff.

The wardrobe in Lucy's bedroom filled steadily.

The only flaw in the smooth achievement of the dressing of Lucy occurred over a certain evening gown that Lucy had seen in an Ackermann Costume Plate: of blue satin, an overdress of net, made with an extremely short waist and the body cut very low around the bust and shoulders. In fact, thought Bennie, one good sneeze would find the whole crumpled around the girl's ankles.

"Entirely out of the question," ruled Althea, called in to arbitrate the discussion, "it is much too daring for a young lady just out."

Lucy turned mutinous. "I would wear this at home."

"In the house?" said Bennie, shocked. "It is not a gown for receiving at home, my dear."

"I meant," said Lucy with scorn, "at home. In India."

"England is your home now," Bennie pointed out.

Lucy crossed to the window and looked out, her shoulders the very picture of rebellion. But when she spoke, her voice was mild. "A married woman could wear such a gown? No matter her age?"

Althea agreed. In her mind, Mr. Cosgrove hovered, and Lucy would likely be married before year's end. There was no harm in painting a bright picture. "A married woman may wear anything she pleased, within reason, of course." And, of course, she added silently, the fashions in Ireland may be more relaxed than in London.

The question of the gown being settled, Althea returned to her own sitting room. She must give a reception to introduce Lucy to their friends, and she had set the date for two weeks hence. She was not quite satisfied, however, with a certain quality in Lucy that might well be called subbornness. When Bennie stopped by on her way down from the sewing room upstairs, Althea begged her to sit down.

"I wonder, Bennie, whether two weeks is sufficient time to let the girl become comfortable here."

"Comfortable? You need not concern yourself with that," said Bennie, an odd note in her voice. "That child will take care of herself."

"Is something amiss? I have not seen much of the girl, and perhaps I have been mistaken in thinking she would not welcome too much attention just at first. Shall we postpone the reception?"

"The child has manners," said Bonnie slowly. "She will not disgrace us. But I should like to see her more elegant in her ways."

"You of all people," smiled Althea, "can instruct her best. I remain grateful every day for your guidance, both when I was growing up and now."

"My dear, you are elegant without even thinking about it. But Lucy—I do not quite know how to say it. She is not precisely biddable."

"Today was not the first of her little rebellions?"

"Far from it. She is grateful for all that is done for her. At least she says so."

"I suppose we must be thankful for that."

Althea turned the conversation then, and various details of the forthcoming reception were decided upon.

But Althea realized that the intrusion of Lucy upon her life was not entirely welcome, perhaps by Lucy as well as herself. Nonetheless, she would do what was required for the girl and be pleased when she married Mr. Cosgrove. Fortunately, that aspect of Lucy's future was in part settled. Tom and Mr. Dedman must handle the legal questions, but the Irish gentleman stood like a fixed point ahead. It was only a matter of arriving there smoothly.

The reception drew near. It was to be only a small affair, but there were innumerable arrangements to be made.

Mr. Cosgrove had called, but Althea suggested that he not press his interest until the party. "Lucy will wish to be in her best looks for you," Althea assured him, with no regard for truth.

A far more persistent caller was Lord Fabyan. Althea's calculatedly cool reception in the long run proved daunting, and Lord Fabyan, a totally ineligible visitor to an unmarried female, since he was formally betrothed, appeared no more. His name appeared on Althea's guest list for the reception. She promptly crossed it off, and thought no more about it.

Althea found herself in the position of a matron of mature years arranging for the presentation of a debutante to a social world to which she herself had been introduced a mere four years before.

"How do they ever do it?" cried Althea wildly on one of the few occasions when she was closeted with Mary

Benbow. Lucy was upstairs in the third-floor sewing room at the moment, apricot satin draped over her hips, being fitted by Miss Hope.

"One thing you must remember," said Bennie prosaically, "is that other ladies, at least if they are launching daughters, have had much more experience than you."

"And one must presume that they have a better acquaintance with their daughters than I have with my niece. I do not know one thought that goes through that child's head."

Bennie murmured understanding.

"I've tried to talk with her. At meals, of course, and whenever I see her. But she seems—she seems as though she is someplace else in her mind. Does it seem so to you?"

"India perhaps. In that case, she will likely recover, once she begins to go to parties and her days are busy. I admit she is not forthcoming," agreed Bennie. "But then, she has been set down in a whirl of activity, and everything must be very new and strange to her." After a moment, Bennie added slowly, "I have wondered whether you have mentioned Mr. Cosgrove to her?"

Althea made a moue. "I confess I do not quite know what to do about Mr. Cosgrove. She has not asked about him, and Tom gave me strict instructions to leave the subject to him. I suppose there are tedious arrangements to be made before the two meet, although I do not quite understand why."

"I think perhaps Mr. Cosgrove might draw her out."

"Certainly, even though their betrothal has not been announced, neither has it been abrogated. I should expect her to betray more curiosity about him than she has. And I have been put to it, I must tell you, to keep Noel Fabyan away from the house, although I believe I have at last succeeded. Lucy is not ready for society yet, and I cannot countenance the visits of any gentleman. Besides, he is completely ineligible."

"Quite right," approved Bennie. "One cannot but fear Lord Soames' reaction when he learns of Lord Fabyan's indiscretion."

"I think," said Althea, "that his interest must have been shallow. I have not heard from Lord Fabyan for three days. Quite a record, I assure you!" Suddenly grave, she added, "Simon's anger will be of no concern of ours, since he would favor Noel with his ill temper—keeping it in his precious family, of course!"

Later, she would recall her words and wonder how she could have been so mistaken.

It was later that day that Althea had her first intimation of shadows moving beneath the surface of her ordered life. Her maid, Pinkham, was brushing her hair into a style of the maid's own, in which she would turn the ends into a cluster of vastly becoming curls at the back of the head, the whole cunningly adorned with feathers of a particularly attractive shade of amber.

"Miss Althea," said Pinkham, "pray hold your head still. How you think I can get these curls to set right if you're always moving around like one of these Punches you see at a street fair, I don't know. Not that you'd seen one there, being fairs are not your style."

"I did see a Punch and Judy," protested Althea, "at the Great Fair in Hyde Park last year."

" 'Course you did. Didn't we all? Not that there's much to see in a Punch and Judy—"

"Pinkham?"

"Yes, miss."

"Why not tell me at once what is on your mind?"

"Me?" Pinkham was all innocence.

"Yes, dear Pinky. When you turn talkative, there's something on your mind. I've noticed you've not been yourself for several days now. What's amiss?"

"It's not my place to say."

That cryptic remark gave notice that the maid was about to point out serious failings on the part of some others of the household. Being lady's maid, she was a cut above the parlor maids and the kitchen staff, but nonetheless she was alert to their faults.

Althea, as usual, intended to make short work of any objections Pinkham might have to carrying tales about the lower orders. "You cannot pique my curiosity, Pinkham, and leave it unsatisfied. I am persuaded that if you have a real problem you will have taken it to Tyson. Clearly you mean me to know about this, so don't give me any more evasions, if you please."

Shorn of roundaboutations, the tale was simple. Molly, the servant chosen to wait on Miss Lucy, had told Pinkham, her eyes wide with mingled shock and excitement, of the daring expedition Miss Lucy had sent her on.

She had been handed a note to deliver, in person, to a certain house on South Audley Street. She was sworn to secrecy as to the addressee and indeed she was unable to read the superscription on the missive.

"And what miss is doing sending her billydoos to anybody, let alone some gentleman in a fancy house, I don't know."

"How do you know it was to a gentleman?"

"Well, a' course she took it to the front door, Molly did. And what would miss be doing anyway, writing to servants!"

It was as well Pinkham's question was rhetorical, for Althea had no answers.

The house Pinkham had mentioned, the house to which Molly was sent secretly with a note from Lucy, was one to bring alarm to Althea's mind.

There could be little question that her niece was shockingly, outrageously in correspondence with Noel, for the address was that of the Fabyan town house.

Althea thought, but only momentarily, of informing Simon of his nephew's behavior in being part of a clandestine correspondence. But she made short shrift of that idea, recognizing it for the reprehensible thing it was: an excuse to see Simon.

She sent Pinkham away. She needed to think. She would not tell Bennie about Lucy's letter. Bennie had enough on her mind without adding a kind of guilt over her charge's outrageous behavior.

There was no need, as it happened, to inform Bennie. The moment her friend stepped inside her sitting room, Althea knew that she had been informed. If Althea found out that Pinkham had spread the gossip, she could promise her maid would regret the talebearing.

Bennie was stricken. At the sight of her miserable expression, Althea's heart sank. "My goodness, Bennie, how gloomy!" she greeted her with false cheer. "We'll stir up the fire and have a good coze."

"Let me do the fire."

"Nonsense. I can certainly manage to poke a log or two."

Bennie's complaint was on the tip of her tongue, ready to spill out. "It's that Lucy," she began, and the whole tale of Molly's errand came out. "And I do not know quite what to do!"

Considering, Althea said, "There is really no choice, is there? The girl must be told she cannot behave with such lack of decency."

"But is it decency she lacks, or simply the knowledge of how to go on? I declare I wish Mr. Cosgrove were here. She could worry him, for a change."

"He's gone to Brighton," said Althea prosaically.

"What on earth for?"

"To see the Pavilion, I presume. Certainly there is nothing like it in Ireland. Or anywhere else, for that matter." She rose. "I shall go to Lucy now. The more I dwell on this behavior of hers, the angrier I shall be."

"I had best go with you," said Bennie. "I mistrust that fire in your eye."

The interview was not a success. Lucy exhibited no sign of guilt when Althea informed her that her correspondence had been discovered.

"Oh! Well, I am sorry, Aunt, that you should have been troubled by such a trifle."

"Trifle! Do you have any idea the disaster that can come of this? Such common behavior! I declare I cannot understand you. Are you courting a scandal?"

"How can there be a scandal over a letter of mere friendship? No one of any sense could object!"

Lucy was being deliberately provocative, thought Bennie. She took a step forward in an attempt to signal discretion to Lucy, but in vain.

"Oh, couldn't they! This kind of behavior, Lucy, may well do in the colonies, but not in London."

Lucy turned abruptly away. "The colonies? There are plenty of very proper English there, I can tell you."

"I wonder," said Althea, ignoring her remark, "how it is that you and Lord Fabyan are on such terms of friendship?"

"Lord Fabyan?" Lucy said innocently. "How do you know I wrote to him? Molly cannot read."

Dryly, Althea said, "You would hardly correspond in such a surreptitious manner with his mother."

"Lucy," said Bennie softly, "you really must not do this kind of thing."

Althea, stirred by mingled dread of scandal and anger, perceived that Lucy appeared undisturbed by Althea's scolding. She went on, trying to make some impression on her. "You are now in a different society. While your father may have indulged you to excess, those days are past. We are trying to teach you how to go on in polite society—"

At last she had reached the girl. She turned on her, sparks flying from violet eyes. "You and your polite society! I know already how to go on, and I am quite sure that a withered-up spinster, who has already grown long in the tooth in the Marriage Market, has nothing to teach me."

"Lucy!" Bennie gasped.

Althea turned white. Lucy's small smile was triumphant. "I understand," she said, dealing blow after blow, "that anyone past the age of twenty-five must put on a cap and retire from society as a misfit. You must not have long to go, dear Aunt!"

Bennie took charge. "You, Lucy, go to your room. I will have something to say to you later—on the subject, among others, of gratitude. Althea, dear, come with me. Now, then, not a word, just come. Bennie knows best."

Not listening to Bennie's soothing words, but sensing the comfort in her voice, Althea, so angry she did not know what she was doing, and in truth incapable of coherent thought, allowed herself to be led to her room. Pinkham appeared as if by magic, when it was merely a question of listening outside doors, and between them they got Althea quieted, with a drink consisting mainly of brandy, and a roaring fire on the hearth to ease her shock.

Bennie said at the door, "My dear, remember that the girl is ignorant beyond belief. She must take after her mother, about whose breeding we have been sadly misled."

8

Later that day, following strenuous representations by Bennie, Lucy was brought to Althea and apologized, at length and very prettily. Althea acknowledged those qualities, although she would not wish to be placed on oath as to the girl's sincerity.

Nonetheless, they must go on, and Althea, essentially generous, did her best to put the ugly incident behind her. She was helped in this resolve by the fact that no scandal had reared its head, and apparently Lucy's letter to Lord Fabyan remained a secret.

But two days passed before Althea felt calm enough to send for Lucy. The girl came in diffidently, Bennie with her.

"Please come and sit down here, opposite me," Althea suggested. "Bennie, there by the fire. I think perhaps we have not explained our plans sufficiently."

"Plans?" echoed Lucy.

The morning light was strong for April, and fell directly on Lucy's face. Dewy, fresh, innocent, Althea thought, but an underlying maturity as well. Perhaps they could all come out of this summer with credit, after all.

"You know about the reception we are giving so you may meet our friends. The invitations have gone out."

Lucy's eyes held an unexplainable look, and then she smiled. "Yes, Aunt," she said demurely. "You are very kind to take the trouble."

Althea, recognizing Bennie's influence, said, "I'm pleased to do so." She had not heard from Tom, and while his instructions were clearly in her mind, she reflected that Tom was not present and she and Lucy quite definitely were. Tom would simply have to take her word for it that his directive was impossible to fulfill. "The family wishes you to come out in society before your marriage."

Lucy started. "Marriage?"

"Of course. He has already spoken to Tom, as the head of the family."

"Then it is all settled!" Lucy's smile this time reached her eyes. She cried ecstatically, "This is magnificent!"

"I am pleased to see that you accept this so well." Althea's tone was dry.

On a confiding note, Lucy said, "I did not think there had been time."

Althea was startled. She exchanged a glance with Bennie, who was equally at sea. Treading delicately and changing the subject tangentially, Althea said, "You may feel you wish to be married directly, but you should have one Season before you go to Ireland."

Lucy's smile faded abruptly. "Ireland? I thought his estates were in Middlesex."

"Middlesex? Oh, no, how can you think so? Ireland."

"No, no! Noel wouldn't lie to me. He said nothing about Ireland."

Stunned, Althea was speechless.

Bennie intervened. "Noel?"

Lucy turned on her. "I think he is styled Lord Fabyan? You met him at the ship. And you, Aunt Althea, spied on my letter. Didn't you read it?"

Althea took a firm grip with both hands on her rising temper and her vanishing self-control. Her anger was directed primarily at Tom for landing her in this mess, when it was Caroline's clear duty to take charge of this dreadful, rebellious, outrageous girl. And where was Tom when his strong sense of propriety and his familial authority, if not his clear head, could be of use?

"And just what," she demanded with dangerous calm, "is Lord Fabyan to you?"

Bennie gestured quickly, but Lucy did not see her, nor would she have correctly interpreted it. "He came aboard at Funchal. He was—very kind."

Bennie said, "But, my dear Lucy, this is impossible."

Lucy turned fiercely to her. "Impossible! What nonsense. I know what he said and how he said it. You were not there."

"But Lord Fabyan is betrothed to Dorcas More!"

Lucy, with ineffable scorn, said simply, "Her!"

"Noel cannot have discussed her with you," said Althea. While she did not like Emma Fabyan particularly, she did believe that Simon's sister would rear her son impeccably. No gentleman would discuss his fiancée with anyone, particularly a stranger.

"It was more the way he said it," conceded Lucy. "But I know he cannot abide her. She is plain, with no more spirit than a new lamb."

"I cannot believe Noel is so ill-bred as to criticize his betrothed."

"Well, she must be plain, mustn't she? For Noel does admire my beauty. He is not the first to do so."

"Nor will he be the last," said Althea astringently. "However, one must not build one's life upon a few shipboard compliments."

"You do not understand," said Lucy, her lower lip thrust out mutinously. "That ninnyhammer will never be Lady Fabyan, with her houses and her own carriage and furs and jewels and parties."

The implication was clear. Dorcas More could never aspire to such felicity, because Lucy Rackham would forestall her.

With a desperate effort to retrieve control of the situation, and to put the discussion upon a more prosaic level, Althea persisted, "I cannot allow this ignoring of contracts."

Pertly, Lucy said, "I do not know about contracts. But I do know that he has signed nothing. He told me so, and he never lies to me."

Nothing Althea could say seemed to reach Lucy. She tried again. Tom might scold, but she could endure that. "I suppose you are referring to Lord Fabyan's contract. I know nothing about his affairs. But I do know that contracts have been signed on *your* behalf."

Lucy took a moment to understand, and then her features went blank, as though a hand had wiped off all expression. The part of Althea's mind not engaged in contemplating the dreadful girl before her thought it interesting that even the sudden lack of animation did not alter the blaze of beauty. Her looks were purely physical, a fortuitous arrangement of nose and eyes, cheekbones, lips, and chin. She was like a Wedgwood vase, perfect in itself but without humanity.

Queerly, Lucy spoke, "On my behalf?"

"Of course. The agreements arranged for your marriage, when you reach nineteen, to Mr. Cosgrove."

In a whisper, Lucy repeated, "Cosgrove?"

Bennie, helpfully, elaborated, "Mr. Claude Cosgrove. Of Ireland."

The words escaped Lucy through ashen lips, against her will, "I never heard of him."

Althea said skeptically, "Truly? I take leave to doubt that. The arrangement was made when you were an infant. Your father must have spoken to you of Mr. Cosgrove."

Lucy recovered, but her eyes were haunted. "Of course. But so long ago I have forgotten."

"You may be sure Mr. Cosgrove has not."

Later, when she and Bennie were alone, Althea said with commendable optimism, "I should not be at all surprised to learn that Lord Fabyan has by now completely recovered from his shipboard romance. He has not called in five days now. Even that idiotic letter did not bring him."

She hugged Bennie and added comfortably, "We

shall have to begin planning Lucy's wedding to Mr. Cosgrove. I have not the slightest hope of Caroline's taking a hand. We have heard the last of this, mark my words.''

9

Althea would have been less sanguine had she been privy to a scene being played out at that very moment in the great hall of Montford Abbey in Middlesex, the country seat of the Fabyans.

There was very little left of the original stone building, the remains being in the form of one upstanding stone wall, broken at the top, the other walls having been removed stone by stone over the centuries to reappear predictably in certain cottage foundations.

The inhabitants of the newer building, a comfortable residence in the style of Queen Anne, were at the moment totally unaware of their surroundings. Lady Fabyan was seated in her favorite chair near the fireplace in which blazed a generous fire. It was no coincidence that the chair bore resemblance to a throne. Her sole subject, as it were—her son, Noel—paced restlessly around the room, driven by an urgency he could not put into words.

His mother was inhibited by no such lack. "Indeed, Noel," she said in her harsh voice, "you've thrown away your common decency, lost your head completely. I cannot conceive what you're thinking of."

"She's an angel," he murmured, "and I love her."

Ignoring the sensibilities of the third person in the room, she continued, "I could better accept some foolish brainstorm over one of the upstairs maids,

Noel. After all, you are a man and therefore prone to such self-indulgence. It's of course an inheritance from your father. Not a female in the county was safe from him." She paused a moment, clearly contemplating with pride the late Lord Fabyan's indefatigable pursuit of *droit du seigneur.* "Undoubtedly inconvenient at times," she added obscurely, "however, I suppose, quite understandable. But, Noel, you cannot abandon your obligations in this manner."

Dorcas More gathered her not inconsiderable courage and spoke for the first time since she had been summoned to this family conclave. "Noel, do not concern yourself with any legalities. I shall not hold you to the b-betrothal agreement."

Both Fabyans turned to stare with astonishment at the girl, as though they had forgotten her, as indeed they had. Lady Fabyan recovered first.

"Nonsense, Dorcas. You and my son are engaged to be married. The advertisement has already appeared in the *Gazette.*" She turned to her son. "I shall not hear of your repudiating it. I should die of mortification."

Noel Fabyan might bear a physical resemblance to his uncle, especially in the breadth of his shoulders and the luxuriant mane of gold-brown hair, dressed in an imitation of Lord Soames' distinctive style. However, the discerning could detect a weakness around the full lips and a certain habit of restlessness in his gaze that were forcefully reminiscent of the late, if unlamented, Lord Fabyan.

Dorcas More saw no flaws in him. "But I shall not mind, Lady Fabyan," she said docilely, "if Noel will be happier with someone else."

"Happy!" Lady Fabyan snorted indelicately. "What, may I ask, has *happy* to do with anything? Marriage has naught to do with happiness, I can tell you." Turning once again to her son, she said, "Am I to assume that your happiness demands marriage with this person—whoever she is?"

"I must have her," he said simply. "I'm sorry,

Dorcas, but I cannot help myself. Maybe I am making a fool of myself, as my mama says, but—I cannot explain it. You see, she is so—so incomparably beautiful."

"I quite understand," lied Dorcas bravely. She had never had any illusions about her own looks, and in truth she was a plain-featured girl. Only an abundance of fine guinea-gold hair and a magnificent pair of dark-blue eyes prevented her from being completely forgettable.

"What will your papa say, Dorcas?" cried Lady Fabyan, more as a gesture than a request for information. Sir Peregrine More was, in Lady Fabyan's opinion, hardly able to say bo! to a goose, even such a meek fowl as his only daughter.

Dorcas, however, was made of sterner stuff than her father. "Who is she, Noel?" she wondered. "Have I met her?"

A flush suffused Noel's tanned skin. "No, she is not yet in society."

Lady Fabyan's attention was caught by an odd note in her son's voice. "Some schoolmiss, then, Noel?" she demanded scornfully. Her voice shook as other possibilities occurred to her for the first time. "Some unacceptable foreigner? I knew it was a mistake to permit you to travel to Italy! Well, speak up, Noel. Who is she?"

Noel could not procrastinate further. He knew his family history. He had been of age, already had succeeded to his father's title, and so had borne the brunt of his mother's furious indignation and resentment when his uncle Simon Halleck and Miss Rackham dissolved their engagement.

Lady Fabyan was much older than her brother Simon, and stood, so she thought, in a maternal relationship to him. Certainly no mother could have been more ferally protective than she when—as she construed it—her darling Simon was thrown over by the young Rackham miss, who, after all, had grown up on the vast Darley estate lying between Montford Abbey and Soames Hall, and should have known Simon well enough to find no surprises in him.

Their mother, the Dowager Lady Soames, had merely laughed at the broken betrothal. "They are of age, Emma," she had told Lady Fabyan at last, "let them alone. I do not care to hear any more on the subject." If she were convinced the estrangement was merely temporary, nothing in her manner revealed it.

Noel thus had reason to fear pronouncing the name of his hoped-for bride. He spoke with trepidation. "Lucy Rackham."

The effect of his audience was not what he expected. No fulminations from his mother, no sighs of jealousy from Dorcas—just a blank stare from the ladies who knew him best.

At length his mother spoke, although in a strangled voice he had not heard before. "*Who?* Do not try to deceive me, Noel, or mislead me. I warn you I will get to the truth of the matter. There is no such person as Lucy Rackham. I know that family, to my cost. The only unmarried female, and deservedly so, is Althea, and Tom's children are still in the nursery. None of them is beautiful, unless your eyes are failing."

She regarded him with the deepest suspicion. "I recall your great-grandfather Fabyan. Mad as a hatter at the end. Fancied himself a curricle, hitched himself up to that old mastiff of his, and drove himself around the park. You're a bit young for lunacy, I should think."

Noel, as always when misunderstood, thrust out his lower lip, giving him the appearance of a headstrong boy in leading strings. "I met her on the *Castle Cliff,* the Indiaman I boarded in Madeira. She was coming here from India, alone. Everyone admired her courage. As well as her beauty."

"Rackham, you say?"

Lady Fabyan mentally turned over the pages of family trees she had stored in her exhaustive memory, and stopped at the pertinent one. She sat bolt upright on her throne chair, and for a moment one could imagine Queen Mary might have looked just so on contemplation of the sins of Bishop Nicholas Ridley. "Good God! You can't mean— I never heard that Edward— He's dead, of course— Noel, tell me, I beg of you to tell me you're not referring to some brat of Edward Rackham's!"

Noel nodded miserably. It was all worse than he expected. He even wished for a fleeting moment he had waited in Funchal for the next ship to call, no matter how many weeks it required, rather than sail home in company with Lucy.

Essentially an overindulged young man, he as a rule had only to insist upon a thing to have it given him. His current plan, to wed the gorgeous Lucy, was clearly meeting serious opposition. However, his desire for the marriage was fixed far more firmly than anything in his life to date. He must have Lucy, no matter how much it cost him. His mother must come 'round in the end. After all, he was the head of the Fabyan family.

Already the first signs of what he read as capitulation could be seen. Lady Fabyan had sat silent and unmoving as stone, once she realized that the angel who had captured Noel's affections was in fact the earthly daughter of Colonel Edward Rackham, who had left England suddenly and without fanfare for other lands. It was noted promptly at the time that his family did not speak of him. Whatever his fault, it had been a serious one. Now the daughter, in all likelihood as flawed as her father, was proposing to become Lady Fabyan. Insult, as it were, added to the injury of Althea's rejection of flawless Simon.

It would not happen, Emma Fabyan silently promised herself, it *must* not happen. The battle with Noel would require all her arsenal of persuasive weapons—no inconsiderable armory. But she had never seen her son quite so stubborn and headstrong as he was now. A superb tactician, Lady Fabyan believed it wise to call upon a piece of artillery not heretofore used. A letter was required, she began to form telling phrases in her mind. But also a certain amount of present privacy was desired.

"Noel," she said in a tone so mild as to cause both young people to look up, startled, "best take Dorcas home. It is too gloomy a day for her to walk." She rose. "I think I shall just lie down for a bit. Your news has quite overset me."

They watched her as she left the room, closing the door quite firmly behind her. They could not hear her quiet instructions to her butler, Fossick.

"I shall want a footman in half an hour—to take a letter in haste to Lord Soames in London."

Noel took the curricle smartly down the drive and turned left at the road. The drive to Dorcas' home would require the better part of half an hour. Dorcas did not know how she could endure such a long silence.

Perhaps, if she simply fixed her mind on a time in the future, a time when all the tumult and the shouting would be over and the new Lady Fabyan installed at Montford Abbey, and the pain and the uncertainty past, she could manage. Her planned mental escape was obstructed.

Once they were well on the road, Noel was impelled to speech. "I'm sorry, Dorcas," he said one more time, as though the iterance of his apology held some magic charm. "I'm glad you don't mind much. It's not as though we ever thought ourselves in love."

In love! her thoughts cried out. But I *was!*

"I never knew what love was before," he confided with an air of satisfaction. "I can't talk about it to anyone but you."

"Perhaps you shouldn't, even to me," said Dorcas equably. She was amazed at her calmness, even though she had been trained not to show open emotion under the most distressing circumstances. Gentlemen did

not like scenes; her governess had told her often
enough to school her tongue. And yet here was a prime
specimen of that mysterious sex, talking as boldly
about his emotions as ever a hysterical miss might do.

He ignored her protest. "I didn't know who she was
at first, but she was the most beautiful person on the
ship. You will like her at once."

She murmured a reply that struck his ear unpleasantly. He might have thought she said, "Only an
idiot would think so," except that such a forthright
statement he considered foreign to Dorcas' very
nature. Nonetheless, he shot a questioning glance her
way and was reassured by the calm expression on her
undistinguished features. She was taking this very
well, he thought with approval, making no scenes or
fruitless demands.

A rather lengthy silence ensued, broken only by the
regular sound of hooves and the monotonous jingle of
harness.

"My mother cut up pretty rough, didn't she? But I
expected that, you know. She has never forgiven Miss
Rackham for throwing my uncle Simon over. That was
before he succeeded to the title. My mother refuses to
have a Rackham in the house, not even Lady Darley,
and she's the daughter of an earl."

"That will make it difficult, then, for the new Lady
Fabyan," said Dorcas pleasantly, "if she is not allowed
to enter Montford Abbey."

Noel would not recognize irony in any case, but as it
was, he was so wrapped up in the marvelous happiness
that had entered his life that he had lost what little
perception he could claim as best.

"Well, you saw how she came 'round," he said cheerfully. "And Lucy will wrap her around her finger."

"She certainly succeeded with you."

Dorcas was in a queer state of mind. Long dis-
ciplined to the outer decorum required of a marriage-
able miss, she had refused to entertain any contrary
thoughts, lest they burst forth at an inconvenient

moment. Now, it was as though her inner chaperone threw up her hands and said, "You've nothing more to lose—I give up." Dorcas could imagine herself uttering uncharacteristically to-the-point remarks. Instead of being mortified, she allowed her fancy full rein. Nothing to lose was right.

Still, there was no need to quarrel. She could feel the beginning of a headache. She assessed the pulsing pain over her right eye and knew the coming attack would be severe. Suddenly she realized that Noel had been talking for some minutes and she had not heeded him. If the burden of his remarks were along the same lines as his previous effusions, it was as well that she had not heard them.

When she began again to listen, he was saying, "She's an angel, a real angel."

Whether it was the incipient headache, the real hurt of his defection, or simple anger at the callousness of his matter-of-fact abrogation of their formal betrothal that moved her, she did not know then, or ever.

She had ridden thus far very calmly, the only signs of perturbation being her hands moving restlessly in her lap. Now, still looking steadfastly ahead, she said, "An angel? Perhaps I have not clearly understood the lessons our vicar has taught us, but until now I should not have expected a heavenly messenger to set about causing disruptions, breaking up family attachments, caring not a fig for other persons' feelings."

Noel, shocked, pulled inadvertently on the reins, causing the horses to veer toward the ditch, nearly upsetting the vehicle. "Dorcas, you don't know what you are saying!"

"Oh, yes, I think I do. Another question that has occurred to me, Noel—that is, it is not precisely a question. I do wonder, you know, how a person would have the temerity to consider himself—or herself for that matter—sufficiently superior to other mortals to merit the affections of an angel."

In a strangled voice, Noel exclaimed, "Dorcas!"

She said no more. In truth her hands trembled
uncontrollably and she thrust them out of sight under
the fur rug covering her knees. She had just made the
longest speech of her life. Surprisingly, her headache
was for the moment lessened, but she knew darkly it
would return, strengthened, later.

They reached her front door in silence. She did not
wait to be helped down. She stood for a moment on the
gravel, again regarding him with the sweet level gaze
he was accustomed to.

"Dear Noel," she said in a tone that was clearly val-
edictory, "I would be pleased to see you happy. Somehow I don't think you are. Don't allow your angel to let
you fall to earth. The landing might be painful."

He could not find words quickly. She hurried up the
steps of her home, the door opened by the footman on
duty as she approached it. She did not look back.

Oddly dissatisfied, Noel set the horses' heads toward
home. What had gotten into Dorcas anyway? All that
talk about the vicar! It was not that Dorcas had any
feeling for him, Noel thought—she'd been as cool as a
fish ever since she'd heard about Lucy.

Now he caught a glimpse of something more, a
shadow moving beneath the surface, and he was
bewildered. Never much given to introspection, he did
not resort to it now. Without any effort at all, he
conjured up the spectacular face of his Lucy and,
whistling to himself, beguiled the journey home to the
abbey.

10

While Lucy was, unwittingly, being discussed at length at Montford Abbey, Althea's house in Grosvenor Square was the scene of much activity.

Preparations for the reception were moving ahead under the tyrannical eye of Tyson. Potted palm trees arrived. Excess furniture departed—but only to the third-floor box rooms, whence they could be easily returned.

Carpets were rolled up and removed. An army of workmen descended to polish the floor for dancing. In and out darted delivery men with hatboxes, glove boxes, caterers' cakes.

Althea was prone to misgivings, some of a substantial nature. The exorbitant cost of Lucy's debut, increased by the need for haste in all the arrangements, would of course be borne by Tom. He had instructed her to do the thing right, and then washed his hands of it.

The actual preparations for the affair gave her no difficulty. Her questions lay more along the lines of the guests.

She had refused at once Lucy's impassioned plea to invite Noel Fabyan, and that, of course, meant she could not invite Lord Soames. While she longed to see Simon, she could not ask him and fail to invite his sister, or Noel. She feared to give an appearance of undue cordiality, moreover, to a man who was no longer interested in her. Sometimes a fire can be brought to life by judicious blowing on the embers, she knew, but she would not stoop to any subterfuge. Not docile enough, she admitted.

And at this point she became irritated in the extreme at Tom. It was his duty to sort out the Cosgrove matter. Get the pair together, arrange whatever needed to be considered, and let everyone know where the matter stood. Tom had directed her at the start not to interfere. In his opinion, marriage settlements were man's work. Arranging the match and all attendant ceremonies were the sphere of womankind.

With firm defiant stroke, she had written the name of Claude Cosgrove at the bottom of her guest list. Now she was subject to doubts. Should she have omitted Mr. Cosgrove until Tom gave her permission?

She had also hesitated over the name of Isobel Morton. She could see the woman in her mind—hair glossy as a raven's wing, striking features, a bold high-bridged nose, and a pair of penetrating dark eyes.

And a wagging tongue. Isobel was an inveterate gossip, and thus was greatly in demand for gatherings, not simply to hear her latest *on-dits*, but also wisely to avoid being the target if she felt herself insulted.

Isobel was rumored to be betrothed to Simon. Now, Althea rightly construed Miss Jenny Burrell's gossip as a figment of her wish to be thought *au courant*. Simon and Isobel, when Althea met them together at Almack's, had not appeared to stand on intimate terms with each other. Of course, the situation could change at any time.

Smiling to herself, she had added Isobel to the list. Miss Morton would be apart from Simon at least for *one* evening!

The day of the reception dawned sunny, with a promise of continued fair weather through the day. Tyson was producing prodigies of work from his under-lings, Bennie had Lucy's apparel and manners in charge, and Althea herself had dealt competently with the list of those to whom cards for the reception had been sent. Although she could not know it, however, disaster was fast approaching from an unsuspected direction.

At first she could not believe Tyson when he announced Lord Soames' presence. "I have put him in the morning room, miss, for the other rooms are unfit."

"Lord Soames! What ever can he want? I am sure I have no wish to see him. Can he be angry because he was not invited?"

She was suddenly panicky over her appearance. Like any green girl, she smoothed her hair with her palm, straightened her skirt, bit her lips to redden them.

She descended the staircase. This was the first time that Simon had entered her own home. On every previous occasion, she had been resident in her brother's household. Her mouth was dry.

The morning room, cheerful and of generous proportions, was dwarfed by the sheer animal force of the man who moved toward her when she came in.

For that first second of meeting, she thought she could discern a certain familiar look in his eye, a look that had been dear to her in the past and had always resulted in the oddest palpitations in the region of her heart, as it did now. The other night at Almack's their meeting had been public. Now, she found her breath coming with difficulty.

After a moment of hesitation, she mastered her feelings and advanced toward him, holding out her hand. She said civilly, "I must apologize. I did not send you a card for tonight."

He bowed over her hand. "Card? Oh, yes, I gather from the obvious clutter that you have some entertainment in train."

"A small reception," she murmured.

"I wish I knew what you were up to," he said.

The years fell away, and once again they faced each

other like two disproportionate game cocks, alert, waiting for an opportunity to slash and wound.

Instantly suspicious of his motives, she demanded, "What do you mean? What am I up to? Such a vulgar phrase!"

"Don't play innocent with me. I know you too well."

She met accusation with coolness. "Perhaps you did at one time, Lord Soames, but I expect we have both altered in the interval."

"Apparently you have changed little. I know of old how cavalierly you treat agreements, contracts, call them what you will."

Striving for reasonableness, she said, "I cannot possibly treat contracts or anything else in any manner until I know what you are talking about."

Simon glared. "You deny you broke our betrothal?"

"Surely, this is well past time to bring that subject to the fore? I thought we had dealt with it. Exhaustively."

"You deny it?"

Hotly, she retorted, "*Yes*, I deny it."

Simon grinned, triumphant. "Then why are we not still betrothed?"

Althea, fuming, cried, "*We* broke it. Together. By mutual consent."

"Together? Ha! Your memory is as faulty now as your judgment was fallible then."

Althea was conscious of a strange sensation. The emotion he aroused in her, she told herself, was anger, but it was nonetheless exciting. She became aware of the blood pounding in her head, her breathing coming quickly and shallowly—in a word, she was alive, as she had not been for months.

There was something under her anger, something that she could not identify until she had leisure some time later to think about it. At the moment, she was compelled to fence further with him, to prod him, perhaps to let him feel the point of her rapier—but that

was too civilized. Indeed, she was shocked to realize
that her vision was much more basic—a delightful
vision of his grabbing her shoulders and shaking her.

He understood her, perhaps too well. "You smile,
Althea. You find our broken engagement amusing?"

"In a way," she said, deliberately provocative.
"After all, it was the last time we thought alike on
anything."

"Then we are to be at odds on this, I assume?"

"Simon, I do beg you. Try to make sense. I cannot
imagine you have come on a day when I really have no
time to visit, in order to berate me over an incident two
years past."

"Incident. I suspected that was all it meant to you!"

Her voice rose in warning. "Simon—"

"Very well. I am informed that your niece is staying
with you." He gestured toward the rest of the house.
In real curiosity, he asked, "How did this come
about?"

"Her arrival was indeed something of a surprise. I
had expected to spend the winter with Bennie in
Italy."

"And she will be with you all Season?"

"I fear so."

"Just who is she?"

In the face of his genuine interest, and because she
had long been in the habit of confiding in him, she told
him.

"I should have expected Darley House to be
opened."

"Caroline does not fancy coming to town."

Simon looked levelly at her. "Your precious family
has, once again, found you of use to them."

Althea sighed. "I really do not wish to discuss it.
Truly there were reasons why I agreed. Bennie is
enjoying herself."

"The pith of it is, though—and do not attempt to
deny it—that Caroline has again refused to come up to
the mark. It is her job to deal with your niece, not

yours." His eyes glittered. "I could make a suggestion—"

Althea, with spirit, retorted, "I have no doubt you could. You have never been at a loss to suggest, but since your ideas tend to run along feudal lines, I believe I should decline to hear them."

Suddenly he gave a burst of laughter. "Wretched girl! How did you guess I was thinking about boiling oil?"

She laughed with him, but said nothing.

No longer laughing, he continued, "You know me too well. Hence you should not have expected to come one over me!"

"Once again, Simon, you explain nothing."

"Very well. I shall put it into simple language. Your niece has taken it upon herself to develop a close acquaintance with my nephew."

Guiltily, Althea remembered all the stir about Lord Fabyan, the strenuous efforts she had been put to, to prevent any interest from being fixed.

He was watching her with fierce attention. "Aha! You do know what I am talking about!"

Suddenly Althea felt a sharp stab of memory that took her breath away. Just so had they stood, glaring savagely at each other, on that day of their bitterest quarrel. But it was not quite the same. For one thing, he had changed. A few silver strands were visible in his thick hair, and a few lines in his face that she did not know.

She knew that she too was altered—her figure more slender, her demeanor calmer.

Simon was waiting. "Well? Are you denying your responsibility?"

Stung, she flung his words back at him. "What responsibility? I have not countenanced any close relationship between any member of my family and any member of yours. I assure you, such an alliance would be as unwelcome to me as it possibly could be to you."

"I remember. You have no need to repeat your loathing of my family, and of me. But it is certainly not the boy's fault—"

"I perceive," she said icily, "you are laying the blame, as usual, upon my shoulders."

"Do you deny that you are encouraging her?"

"Simon, you have not changed in the least. If there is a bad situation at hand, we may trust you to make it worse. Of course it is my fault. How can you doubt it? I should somehow have known—and I cannot imagine why I failed to make myself acquainted with the facts —that Lucy, of whose existence I was unaware a month ago, would travel on a ship I knew nothing of, and so beguile a young man of no fixed scruples into . . . whatever she may have beguiled him into."

Her sarcasm had reached him. She was gratified to see his features suffused with a dusky flush. He was ready, judging from the flexing of his fingers, to lay violent hands on her.

To her own surprise, she was not at all loath to feel his hands on her, even violently, as seemed likely.

All he could find to say, however, was to point out, fiercely between clenched jaws, "You have twisted my words. I certainly do not mean to indicate that you are at fault, at least in such a way."

"Then in some other way?"

Whatever he might have said was in a moment gone. The door opened abruptly and Lucy burst in.

"Miss Benbow says I may not wear my new saffron gown tonight, and I have—" Her voice died away as she caught sight of Simon.

"Lucy, one must knock before opening a closed door. Lord Soames, may I present Miss Lucy Rackham?"

Oh, no, she thought, not Simon too! For Lord Soames was staring, obviously much struck by the peach-bloom complexion, the delicately arched brows, the straight little nose—and the huge violet eyes fringed in dark lashes, eloquent of innocence and just now holding immense admiration.

She curtsied, blushing in confusion, and stammered a word or two. Althea thought, The girl looks five years younger than when she arrived.

In a moment Althea had sent her upstairs, promising to look into the question of the saffron gown. "Well, Simon," she said wickedly, recalling his remarks to her at Almack's, "you think this young lady is docile enough?"

He turned to her as though brought back from a distance. "Docile? Good God, that's the last thing she is! I can see what struck Noel all of a heap."

"Indeed?"

"Let us hope he soon comes to his senses."

She accompanied Simon to the door. "But, Simon, you think he might not?"

"All I'm sure of, Althea," Simon said in a surprisingly savage voice, "is that you should have left the country before letting that sister-in-law of yours burden you with *that* young lady. You haven't any idea of the trouble you're heading into."

"Are you threatening me, Simon? I assure you that if there is any kind of trouble, I shall deal with it." She was disappointed and vaguely hurt that his visit had resulted only in a renewal of hostilities. She was moved to add, "And in any case, I wonder that Lord Fabyan does not send you to mind your own affairs, which at the least seem not to march to perfection. He is of age, is he not? Pray do not tell me he has sent you to treat with me, for I shall not believe you."

"Then I shall tell you no such thing," he shouted, heedless of the butler hovering in the hall and the sudden cessation of sounds from the workmen in the salon. "You have outdone yourself in stubbornness this time!"

11

The first guests were arriving. Althea had placed Lucy at her right hand. The saffron gown had been set aside for a later and more spectacular party—so Althea had suggested, winning the battle by this device—and the debutante was fetchingly garbed in pale pink with an overskirt of gauze, and Althea's pearls, lent to her for the occasion.

Bennie had begged off standing in the receiving line, saying she was tired.

"Just a wee bit, Althea. I am fine, of course, but I do think standing too long might be too much for me."

Instantly concerned, Althea looked with affection on her dear friend. "I have let you do too much, dear Bennie. Now that Lucy is about to be out in society, you shall have more time to rest. Are you—you are *not* suffering a relapse of that indisposition of the winter? Shall you want to return to Bath?"

"No, my dear. You are excessively kind to offer. But truly London is much more lively than Bath. And I am really quite well."

"Perhaps. But I fear Lucy has been a handful for you, as Tom promised she would be."

And Simon too, for that matter. Only this morning he had predicted darkly that trouble lay ahead. Although he had indicated that he himself might be the source of such turbulence, yet Althea could agree that Lucy was far from a delight in her house.

As is usual on such occasions, the steady stream of arrivals, once the hour had come, induced in Althea a kind of hypnotic state. Lord and Lady Hatton were among the first to come, followed shortly by Miss Jenny Burrell, Mr. Otis, Lord Carroll, Sir Horace Wychley, who lingered long with Bennie, Lord Fairbank and his lady, all saying the correct things, pausing for a stunned instant—or longer on the part of the gentlemen—as they received the impact of violet eyes and flawless complexion.

Althea would have been less than human if she had not soon perceived herself as exceptionally plain, in such a direct comparison with the miss who was certain to be the talk of their world on the morrow.

Althea glanced toward the entrance, wondering how many were still coming. Suddenly, she stiffened. The little knot of guests at the door eddied and parted, and from their midst emerged Noel Fabyan.

She heard a pleased little gasp from Lucy, standing beside her. "Oh, please, Aunt Althea, don't be angry!"

"He comes to a house where he is not invited? In fact, I have sent him away more than once. This is very ill-bred of him!"

Lucy, looking across the throng toward Noel with ill-concealed delight, murmured, "But, Aunt, he *was* invited."

Althea, a fixed smile on her features, said, "What!"

"I sent him a card."

Bennie was standing nearby, Sir Horace at her side. She could not overhear the exchange between Althea and her niece, but she must have caught sight of Noel at the same moment Althea had. She caught Althea's eye. In Bennie's expression Althea read, as though in plain print, the cause behind the drawn expression that worried Althea. A handful and a half!

Well, Althea would deal with this obstreperous child, but in the morning. She would be in better control of her temper by then, and after all, no real harm was done.

Noel had reached them, and bent over Althea's hand, which she automatically offered him, and smiled boyishly at her.

"How good of you to relent and invite me, Miss Rackham. I quite feared I was in your bad graces!"

He was not welcome, but she dared not tell him so, not with Miss Jenny's bright birdlike eyes watching from across the way and Isobel Morton not far distant. But the boy was not going to emerge scot-free.

"How delightful to see you, Lord Fabyan. And Miss More? Is she not with you? I was interested to see the notice of your betrothal!"

She was gratified to see a slow flush inch up his cheeks. "Dorcas finds the country more to her taste at this time of the year. I have just returned from the abbey and left her very well indeed."

He did not seem to know that his uncle had visited her that morning on his behalf. Althea did not intend to enlighten him. Whatever socially correct answer she might have given him, he would not have heard, she realized, for his attention was now fixed on Lucy, and the rest of the world forgotten.

She thought she heard him murmur to Lucy, "I have told them about us."

If she had thought earlier that Simon was greatly exercised over a trifle, she was now undeceived. Noel was indeed serious in his intentions concerning Lucy. What a coil! Lucy betrothed to Mr. Cosgrove, whom she said she never heard of; Lucy hanging out clearly for Noel, who was betrothed to Dorcas, who was— It came to Althea that she had only the slightest acquaintance with Dorcas More.

It might be well to remedy that lack.

Later in the evening, when Lucy had left her aunt's side to join the dancing in the second drawing room, Althea surveyed the scene from just inside the foyer. From here she could hear the musicians at a distance, the high hum of conversation punctuated at frequent intervals by an explosion of laughter. She recognized Miss Morton's fluting and distinctive three-note laugh. From the dining room came clink of cups and tinkle of crystal.

"All in all," she said comfortably to Bennie, who had just joined her, "the party seems to be a success."

"Indeed it is," said Bennie. "Lucy dances very well. Earlier I was watching the dear young people."

"Bennie, you know that Lucy deliberately disobeyed me and send a card to Lord Fabyan. I declare I do not know quite what to do with her. Ignorance I may accept, for that may be remedied, but rebellion—"

After a moment, when Althea did not say any more, Bennie said, "Just the same, she and Lord Fabyan make a nice-appearing couple. You really should watch them."

"Handsome is," said Althea repressively, "as handsome does."

Suddenly Althea realized she had not seen Lucy for some time. She had supposed she was dancing with the others. She turned to Bennie. "When did you see them dancing?"

"Some time back," she answered. "Just after Lord Fabyan arrived." Struck by Althea's expression, she added, "Oh, no. It is impossible. Even if Lucy doesn't know better, certainly Lord Fabyan must."

"You have more confidence in Lord Fabyan's sense of the proprieties than I do, for she has him completely in thrall. Let us pray you have the right of it. Do you search those rooms, and I will go this way."

With an effort of will, she managed to move with indirection—instead of storming—through her rooms, looking for Lucy. She was not in sight. Catching Bennie's eye at the dining room door, she saw by the faint shake of Bennie's head that Lucy was not in the crowded rooms Bennie had traversed. Where could the wretched girl be?

Althea moved toward the stairs, thinking Lucy might have felt faint and gone to her room to rest for a few moments. Then she saw the door on the far side of the second drawing room open, and Lucy, wearing an expression of guilt touched with extreme pleasure and some triumph, slipped in. In a moment she was followed by Lord Fabyan. He averted his eyes from the company, perhaps in the belief that if he could not see the others, they could not see him. His cheeks were flushed too, but Althea saw no triumph in him—only a mixture of embarrassment because of the offense he had committed against his breeding, and satisfaction at whatever had gone on in the garden.

Althea stood rooted to the floor in disbelief, a vessel full of wrath. What could she do, outside of chaining the minx to the bedpost? Confinement to the house, of course, would be the least punishment that she intended to inflict on her niece on the morrow. But she began to realize that Lucy was an inventive girl, having more strings to her bow than were readily apparent. How could a girl of only eighteen be so devious?

The door, as everyone knew, opened onto the garden, and it was abundantly clear to Althea that the pair had escaped the heat of the crowded room and enjoyed a few moments in the cooler air of the dark garden. Alone, quite alone.

The fact was also abundantly clear to at least one other person. Isobel Morton's three-note laugh sounded softly in Althea's ear. She turned to look directly into Isobel's dark, vastly amused eyes. There was nothing for Althea to say.

Isobel would likely do all the talking, and on the morrow Lucy, as well as Althea, would have no shred of reputation remaining.

12

The rest of the fateful evening went past Althea as though behind a glass barrier. She knew people were making their farewells; she believed she must be saying the correct things, for none of them looked askance at her; the musicians departed, and at last she and Bennie and the disgraced Lucy were together, alone.

Lucy, wisely, seemed everything that was demure and apologetic. "Dear Aunt, I fear I have done something very bad this time?"

"You may say so."

"But the room was so hot, you know. And I asked Lord Fabyan to escort me into the garden, only for some fresh air. We were gone only a few moments."

"Do you consider a quarter of an hour only a few moments?"

Lucy looked pityingly at her. "But what could have happened in fifteen minutes? And besides, nothing did."

"Nothing, except your reputation ruined, Lord Fabyan revealed to be a man of no scruples and very few principles, and I doubt I have enough credit to carry it off. I shall send you to Darley Hall and recommend to my brother that the most stringent supervision must be applied."

"Aunt! You cannot be so cruel!"

"Cruel? I fear my fault lies in having been much too indulgent."

Lucy turned to Bennie, whom she considered her ally. "Miss Benbow, please help me. Tell my aunt I am sorry."

"My dear," said Bennie gently, but gravely, "I fear that a mere apology will not mend the situation. You have truly outraged us all."

Whether Lucy was excessively fatigued or worried, or whether Althea was, rightly, more depressed than she had been since Simon's default, it seemed to Althea that Lucy's level gaze held no remorse. If this girl were a mere eighteen, Althea was sadly deceived. It occurred to her that Edward had lost no time upon his arrival in India nearly twenty years before in establishing, if not a marriage, at the least a liaison. Perhaps marriage came later.

Good God, she thought, I am sponsoring an illegitimate child! Her resentment of her brother and sister-in-law on the subject of Lucy knew no bounds.

Bennie was saying, smoothing ruffled waters, "Perhaps everything will look brighter in the morning. Should not Lucy go upstairs to bed at once?"

Althea nodded. When, after a few minutes, she and Bennie went up together, Althea said only, "Brighter in the morning? Bennie, you are a dear optimist. But let us both look on the cheerful side of it. Things could hardly look worse!"

Inevitably, Althea realized, one of the first callers on the morning after the party would be Lord Soames.

This time, however, she was no longer to be routed by a surprise attack. She knew, none better, where Simon was vulnerable. He might say he wanted a docile bride. He would expire, she considered, of boredom, were he to be unfortunate enough to get his wish.

She knew, too, that a man passionate and impulsive in rage would be—indeed had been—equally passionate in love. She had been alive, embracing all of life with incomparable zest, when Simon was the focus of her emotions. There was nothing pale or drab about Simon.

If there existed a chance to win him back, she must take it.

She went down to him in the morning room. The other rooms were noisy with dismantling of the party arrangements and the restoration of the usual furniture to its accustomed place.

She found him pacing back and forth across the small room like one of the lions in the Tower. In fact, with his graceful stride and his mane of tawny hair, the suggestion of latent strength in his carriage, he resembled the Tower felines more than a little. If Simon had been indignant on his previous visit, he was now enraged.

"You wish to see me?" she inquired warily.

He paused in his pacing and glared at her. "Indeed I do. I cannot believe such depravity does not appear in your features."

"May I suggest that you mind your manners, Lord Soames?"

"My manners have nothing to do with it. Yours, however, leave much to be desired."

It was very odd, she thought, that when he is standing this near to me, I forget that miserable Lucy and the dreadful consequences of her stupidity, and I can only remember—

His words slashed at her. "Totally lost to decency. You have deliberately defied my wishes."

So much for sweet memory. "Your wishes?" she echoed tartly. "What have your wishes to do with me?"

"You deliberately invited Noel to your reception, fully aware of his ineligibility. You cannot have forgotten his betrothal!"

"If he has forgotten it, as one might gather from his actions, it is little wonder I do not hold it in the forefront of my thoughts."

He stared at her, his powerful chest moving with his

shallow, angry breathing. "You cannot be abetting this infatuation of his?"

"Your wishes, I believe you said, when you accused me of thwarting them. What about Noel's wishes?"

"His family's wishes must be paramount in this matter. Miss Lucy seems to be ignorant or contemptuous of all standards of decorum. It is no more than I might expect—"

"From a Rackham, you were about to say? No doubt the Fabyans have a monopoly on perfection. By the way, how is Miss More faring?"

"Miss More?" he echoed, blankly.

"Lord Fabyan's fiancée," she reminded him kindly.

"I warn you—" He was obviously ready to explode. "Change your abandoned ways, my girl, or I shall change them for you. Don't think I can't—"

She interrupted with the air of one who has not been listening. "I do admire your neckcloth. Of your own design, I think? By next week we shall be entertained by a plethora of shabby imitations."

He was stopped in full spate. His vanity, a quality she knew well, responded for a full minute. "Do you think so?"

Then, eyeing her pleasant expression with misgiving, he recovered, but his anger had become diffused. He sent her a glance that told her he had recognized her game. There was respect for her, as well, as a worthy antagonist. In an altered voice, he said, "You haven't heard anything I said."

"On the contrary," she assured him. "I was hanging on every word. It is not often that anyone rings such a peal over me, and I must admit that you have invented a few accusations that I have not heard before." In an effort to make her meaning clear, she added, "At least, not directed at me."

"Such as?" he demanded.

"I believe you accused me of having no sense of decency? Perhaps, Lord Soames, you have confused me with one of the Cyprians of your acquaintance. You will recall we have spoken of this in the past. Remembering our conversation on that head, one might imagine that you admired that quality."

Gratified, she saw he was too furious to speak. She continued, in a confiding manner, "How did you learn about your nephew's sad lapse from propriety? I suspect Miss Morton is having a busy morning."

The flush on Simon's cheek told Althea she was right. Isobel had lost little time, and in all likelihood Simon was her first confidant.

Simon's grin was savage. His eyes kindling, he retorted, "I might have known you would not fight fair."

Deliberately defiant, Althea faced him. Her head throbbed from a sleepless night, and to add to her discomfiture, she knew he was right. That wretched, dreadful girl!

"Let us understand each other, Lord Soames. I am not responsible, thank God, to you. You have lost any right you may once have had to dictate to me on the subject of my behavior."

"I never found any fault in your behavior," he said, reasonably for a change. "I disapprove, with reason, of your abominable family, who kept you constantly at their beck and call, running their errands. Everything Caroline didn't want to do, you did. She turned you into a nursemaid."

She began to feel quite deliciously stimulated. He too had forgotten nothing that had passed between them. If he had no feeling remaining for her, surely he would be dismissed at least the details from his mind?

"Is that all?" she demanded, with an appearance of hauteur.

"Except for your idiotic assumption that I maintained a harem on the side," he said, turning savage with remembered injustice.

Diverted, she fell into the trap. "You never denied it."

"I saw no need to."

Then, regretfully pulling back from a full exploration of bygone injuries, she recalled the subject before them. "I may in time change my ways—but only if I choose. Certainly, not at your behest, no matter how cogently, or insultingly, presented."

Returning to the fray, Simon demanded, "Then you persist in this malevolent scheme of yours of pushing Lucy into Noel's arms, no matter that he is already promised to Miss—whatever her name is?"

Althea smiled, a secret, enigmatic smile, which had the desired effect. Simon responded like a wounded lion.

"I see you set yourself up in the position of adversary. Be very sure, Miss Rackham, that you are not digging a pit for your own destruction!"

She smiled again, this time with tranquillity. "How scriptural!" She rose and gestured in the direction of the door, looking with feigned disinterest at him. "Have you quite exhausted your store of calumnies? I do hope so, for I confess this conversation begins to weary me."

He stormed from the room in a great cloud of anger and disapproval. Were it not for Tyson's alert presence in the hall, Lord Soames would have slammed the door resoundingly.

Simon's last words echoed in her ears. "You have not seen the end of this!"

She smiled happily to herself and murmured, "I certainly hope not!"

13

Dorcas More, in spite of Noel's assurance to Althea, was not in the least happier in the country. In truth, she had never been more miserable in her life.

Her father was aware that his Dorcas was wretched, and as fathers will, he laid the blame squarely on the shoulders of her intended bridegroom. Sir Peregrine More bided his time, expecting the suspected lovers' tiff to be soon made up. But since Dorcas' spirits grew daily heavier, he decided it was time to intervene.

He searched her out in the small sitting room she had appropriated for her own use. She was looking out at an unseasonably cool day for early May. The clear greens of new leaves were softened by showers, with a soft blurriness that pleased the eye but dampened the spirits.

Sir Peregrine was not, as Lady Fabyan believed, a lackwit. Her view of him was colored by his clear dislike for her, a dislike that made him indifferent. Lady Fabyan was seldom happy if she were not the center of admiring attention.

He did not precisely like the marriage arranged between his only daughter and young Lord Fabyan, whom he considered something of a milksop, but the pair had known each other since leading-string days, and if Dorcas had set her heart on him, then her father meant her to have him.

He now entered Dorcas' sitting room quietly and

stood beside her before she was aware of his presence.

"Oh, Papa! You startled me!"

"Dreaming, were you, pet? I make no doubt you were planning your wedding gown. Your aunt spoke about September as a likely time."

His words were light and teasing, but his dark eyes were entirely serious. He had a fairly good grasp of how things were between his daughter and Noel, not the least because he had not seen Noel around the house for a week and he had heard only this morning that he had gone up to London.

Dorcas turned to him. Her eyes were red, even the tip of her small straight nose was rosy, and the tears that now threatened to overflow were not the first. "I think not, Papa. There will be no wedding."

"That Fabyan lad," said Sir Peregrine wisely. "Lost his senses, I shouldn't wonder." Attempting a light tone, he offered, "Want me to call him out?"

His raillery had the desired effect. Dorcas' laugh, though strangled, was nonetheless present. "I don't suppose you've decided he won't do?" her father asked. "No? Too much to hope for, I fear."

"I know you don't like him, but he's really very kind. When he wants to be."

Sir Peregrine frowned. Could the cub think his Dorcas not worth the effort to be kind? If he, Peregrine More, were twenty years younger, he *would* call him out.

Since he could not turn back the clock, he put his arm around her shoulders and drew her to the love seat. "Come, my dear, sit down and tell me about it."

It took some few minutes before the whole situation lay bare before him. Young Noel had formed a new attachment. Sir Peregrine was well informed about the reputation of the late Lord Fabyan, and the son's inconstancy, therefore, came as little surprise. But the worrying part of it was that the new attachment was no country wench who could be wooed, won in a manner of speaking, and then discarded. Lady Fabyan and Sir Peregrine were in harmony on this head.

A young Rackham lady, so Dorcas informed her father. This connection, he concluded, must be of a formal nature, and marriage was inevitable. And where did that leave his daughter? As a matter of fact, if he were only *ten* years younger . . .

He recalled with some irritation the time he had spent—wasted, so it seemed—arranging the settlement to be Dorcas' upon her marriage. There were a wealth of papers secured at this moment in his library safe—papers of the estates that Sir Peregrine was putting in Dorcas' name, for example. His own wealth he was dividing, a third of it earmarked for Dorcas now. He believed it wise for Dorcas to have sufficient funds to enable her to leave her husband, if she wished. The other two-thirds, of course, would be hers upon his own death. None of these arrangements would leave Sir Peregrine in poverty. He had more than ample to meet his needs.

The troubling aspect was thus not Dorcas' security. The arrangements had been made in good faith, after young Noel had given every assurance that he was irrevocably attached to Dorcas. That was only a week before he had left England to travel abroad. Suppose his infatuation with the Rackham girl died quickly and Noel and Dorcas weathered this particular storm. What about the next time? And there would be a next time, he was certain of that. The Fabyans were no models of constancy.

The agreements, the legal papers in the safe, the undertakings both formal and verbal—all these made what was the basic of a settled, secure life. Without adherence to commitments, all would be chaos.

He knew that Lady Fabyan considered him a nonentity. In this, she was, as in so many other things, wrong.

Doing nothing more effective at the moment than absently patting his daughter's shoulder, as soon as he repaired to his study he sat at the desk, a frown between his eyes and his lips tightened, and wrote a letter. In three days his effort was rewarded.

"Your aunt wishes you to visit," he told Dorcas, holding up the letter.

"In Mount Street?"

"Of course."

"Papa, you want to be rid of me? I know I have not been the best company."

Her forlorn expression wrung his heart. "Now, my dear, I shall even perhaps come to visit myself."

"Oh, Papa! How splendid. Shall we go together?"

At once regretting his impulsive offer, he retreated. "Not just at once. Let me read you a bit here from Eleanor."

His sister lived in London, in a large, even grand, house. Lady Barnett was not a favorite with Sir Peregrine if it came to a question of constant company, but nonetheless he had always found her reliable in a crisis. She had not failed him now.

" 'Dear Dorcas,' she writes, 'will find much to keep her busy. I shall enjoy taking her around. I shall doubtless find my own youth restored in her company.' "

"But, Papa," objected Dorcas.

"Wait, my dear, there is more. A new man or two in town, she writes. One from Ireland, fancy that. Well furnished with funds she says." Sir Peregrine wondered whether his plan was sound. Suppose Dorcas took a fancy to the Irish gentleman. Who in the world would want to live in Ireland? He had no very clear idea of the country, but he had heard sufficiently to resolve never to travel there. But if Dorcas removed in that fashion, he might have to sacrifice himself more than he wished.

"Will it not look as though I am running after Noel if I follow him to London?" Dorcas inquired.

"Certainly not!"

"I am relieved. I should not like to be forward."

Sir Peregrine considered. Then, unanswerably, he asked, "Why not?"

Perhaps, she thought, she had not been forward enough. Surely she did not quite like to sit docilely by while Noel raved about angels and speaking violet eyes. Especially, she added, when he had told me more than once that he admired her "quiet, unassuming looks." Did he indeed? Then how could it be that he had fallen head over heels with a spectacular beauty?

With Papa's encouragement, she thought, surprising herself, Forward? Why not, indeed!

Althea received the news of Miss More's arrival in London in the form of an invitation to cards from Lady Barnett. "Look, Bennie," she said at breakfast, "Lady Barnett is stirring herself in society. I have not seen her in months. I understand she never goes out."

Bennie told her, "She was at Lady Hatton's the other afternoon. You were not present—I think riding in the park. I spoke to her. Of course she does not go out much, for she does not dance. The accident to her foot left her with a sad limp. But you say she is entertaining?"

"Indeed she is. An evening of cards, and"—Althea frowned over the invitation—"in honor . . . Bennie, she is entertaining in honor of— My goodness!"

Bennie stopped in the act of putting marmalade on her bread. In a moment, she smiled, having traced the connection she sought. "Lady Barnett was a More before she married. I believe she is aunt to Miss Dorcas More."

"I shall never be able to baffle you, shall I? Yes, indeed, it is Miss More who is to be honored." After a few moments, she resumed in an altered tone, "But what puzzles me more than that Noel's betrothed has come to town to this: it has been almost a week since that disastrous reception we gave for Lucy, and I see no lack of invitations coming in, even a number for Lucy. Can it be that Isobel Morton, for the first time in her life, held her tongue?"

"It seems scarcely credible," agreed Bennie. "Especially on an incident so shocking!"

"I shall begin to believe in miracles, I believe."

"I think I shall allow Lucy to accept an invitation or two, just to see how she goes on. Do you think she is chastened sufficiently?"

"I doubt there exists sufficient punishment. But I do agree. It is your purpose, after all, to introduce her to society."

"But in such a way, Bennie!"

"Wait and see," her companion counseled. "Shall you go to Lady Barnett's?"

"Indeed I shall. The invitation includes you."

"I think, unless you wish me very badly to go, I shall remain at home."

"A little tired, Bennie?" inquired Althea, at once full of concern. "Did I hear you coughing this morning?"

"Only a little. But I shall expect to hear everything about the young lady. I have a great curiosity about Miss More."

"I too. Do you suppose that Noel, faced with the fiancée he has neglected, will recollect his obligations?"

"If he does, I hope Miss More will think twice about taking him back," said Althea vigorously. "She is not like an old glove, after all, to be discarded at will. I remember his saying to Lucy that night"—no need to specify which night she meant—"that he had told them at home. I do hope he has not totally burned his bridges."

The news of his fiancée's arrival in London came to Noel as an unrelished surprise. Indeed, he was, in all likelihood, the last man in London to be informed of Dorcas' whereabouts. He felt pursued, as Dorcas had foretold. Couldn't they realize, he stormed in the privacy of his study in the Fabyan town house, that the love of the ages had come to him? He merely wanted to be left alone, to savor his feelings for Lucy, to feast his eyes on her beauty, and to know that she thought him an unparalleled suitor?

In pursuit of this overriding purpose of his, he repaired to Althea's house on Grosvenor Square. It was there that the first intimations trickled down to Noel that Dorcas' presence in London might prove to be more than a simple unpleasant and temporary disruption in his hallowed pursuit of bliss.

Althea had been informed that Noel's alliance with Miss More had been broken, by mutual consent, and he was now allowed to call on Lucy, under close supervision.

On this particular day, Mr. Cosgrove was of the company, as was Sir Horace. Lady Hatton was just leaving, and met Noel in the foyer.

"How base of you, Lord Fabyan, not to tell us that your fiancée was in London!"

"My apologies, ma'am," he said automatically.

"I shall have to entertain for you," she said gaily. "Tell me when would be the best time! Some afternoon at cards? Do ask Miss More, and I shall call on her in a few days."

"I beg of you—" he began, and stopped short, seeing belatedly where his remark would take him.

"Beg of me what?" prompted Lady Hatton when he did not continue.

"Go to so much trouble for—for us."

It was a lame recovery, he thought with a sinking feeling. He must learn to do better if he were not to come to disaster. At bottom an easygoing young man, without strong determination in any direction, he was conscious for the first time of a niggling suspicion that the future held more obstacles than he welcomed. Not ordinarily fanciful, he was moved now to consider his pursuit of happiness as a steeplechase—Lucy the clearly visible steeple toward whom his race was set, a goal to be reached in spite of every obstacle rising in his path.

It was as a shaken man that he stepped into Althea's drawing room and fixed his eyes, like a lodestar turning to the north, on the incomparably beautiful features of Lucy Rackham.

* * *

Lucy had received, through some devious scheme of Lady Barnett's, an invitation of her own to the card party. Althea was of two minds about allowing her to go. However, on the principle of getting the worst of it over with, she was prepared to accede to Lucy's request.

Lucy did not ask Althea's permission to go. She knew she was not in such great disgrace as she had been just after the incident at the reception. She was consequently a little easier with her aunt than previously, rather in the way of the mutual regard of survivors of shipwreck.

At length, Althea broached the subject.

"I do not care to go," said Lucy indifferently. "An evening of cards? With Lady Barnett? I met her, you know, when Miss Benbow and I drove in the park. She looked at me so, I thought I should freeze to death."

"And why should you not go, Lucy? I am persuaded there will be many in company. And Lady Barnett cannot dislike you, for she did not need to invite you. Certainly you would see many of your acquaintances."

"The invitation read 'to meet Miss More,' did it not? I am not so stupid as not to know who she is. I shall not allow her in my house in the future, so why should I wish to meet her now?"

Althea was appalled. "My dear child, I cannot seem to convince you that you are in danger of receiving a disastrous setback. I know I have allowed Lord Fabyan to call. Not to further your pretensions, but for reasons of my own."

Indeed she had expected Simon to return to the battle. He had promised that she had not heard the end of the affair, and she anticipated the next stage with some eagerness. So far, he had not returned.

Lucy smiled enigmatically. "No setback, Aunt Althea. I know precisely what I am doing."

Althea's temper frayed. Althea thought, I shall never understand what this girl thinks! "And what are you doing? You seem so certain that your future lies with Lord Fabyan. Have you the slightest notion of the obstacles to overcome before your way is smooth? Surely," she added as an unwelcome possibility struck her, "surely there is nothing fixed between you two?"

Lucy was slow to answer. "Not precisely. But I merely have to crook my finger, thus, and Lord Fabyan, or anyone else I choose, will offer for me."

"Anyone else? What do you mean?"

"As you have pointed out, Aunt, I must meet many eligible suitors before I make up my mind. At the moment, however, I fancy Lord Fabyan."

Unsuccessfully trying to hide her exasperation with the smug girl, Althea pointed out, "You must obtain permission from my brother before any arrangements can be made. And Mr. Cosgrove—I explained to you his position."

Indeed she had. Mr. Cosgrove had exhausted the charms of the Regent's Pavilion and had returned from Brighton last week. He had come promptly to call, but to Althea's surprise, he had not pressed his suit with Lucy. In truth, Althea suspected that he among all the men in London had not fallen under the spell of Lucy's beauty.

"Mr. Cosgrove's position," scoffed Lucy. "He has none at all, at least with me. I shall not be *Mrs.* Anybody. I shall be *Lady* Somebody, and there is nothing you can say to make me change my mind."

Dryly, Althea suggested, "It is customary to wait until you receive an offer."

"As you did? For two years you have been waiting to be offered for again. You see, Noel has told me about you and Lord Soames. You see how much good waiting did for you. No, thank you, Aunt. I have no wish to follow in your footsteps."

White with hurt, Althea said softly, "No one asks you to do that."

Lucy smiled archly. "In fact, Noel has told me a great deal. Lord Soames—did I not meet him once here? The day of the reception. A very attractive man, Aunt Althea. Too bad you whistled him down the wind!''

She was gone before Althea could begin to say what she thought. How common! How vulgar her remarks about Simon! How right she was!

The realization that Lucy had put her finger on Althea's most vulnerable weakness did nothing to put her in charity with the girl.

She was torn between disgust for Lucy and a desire either to throttle her or to send her to Caroline to do with what she would. A dungeon would not be too harsh, but unfortunately Darley Hall was a modern residence.

Slowly the thought came to Althea, The minx means to be Lady Somebody. Good God, she could not mean *Lady Soames!*

14

The card party in honor of Dorcas More was done in style. When Lady Barnett put her mind to it, as she had upon receiving an informative letter from her brother, she was one of the noteworthy hostesses in London.

The modest term "card party" belied the reality. The affair spread through five rooms, in addition to two supper rooms. By the time Althea arrived, the party was in full swing.

She had requested Mr. Cosgrove to escort her. She had come to like him for his imperturbable poise. "And besides," she had told him, "you will have an opportunity to meet Miss More."

"I shall be delighted," he told Althea. "She is Lord Fabyan's betrothed? I confess I cannot quite understand why he spends so much time in your drawing room, Miss Rackham. I do not mean to be critical, but some of your customs seem illogical to me."

"You are quite right," she assured him. "This particular affair seems illogical to me too. It is not an expected thing for Lord Fabyan to ignore his fiancée, as you have seen that he does."

But better Lord Fabyan underfoot on Lucy's account, she told herself, than—for instance—Lord Soames! She had spent more than one sleepless night since Lucy had indicated that her ambition might fly higher than Lord Fabyan. The girl had met him only once, the day of the reception, when she had burst into the morning room with a question about the saffron gown. Unless she had met him at one of the other modest entertainments she had frequented? Althea realized that she was afraid to ask Lucy—*afraid* of that slip of a girl!

They arrived at Lady Barnett's to find the house already crowded. Noel, to her surprise, stood subdued and unwilling beside his fiancée in the receiving line. Beyond him, Althea saw Emma Fabyan, obviously come up to town for this event, possibly to keep Noel in line.

He spoke very briefly to Althea and only a word to Claude Cosgrove. He looked over her shoulder as though expecting to see Lucy. Indeed, she would not have known him for the same smitten swain who languished in her drawing room.

Dorcas, dressed simply but handsomely in deep-strawberry crepe, dimpled prettily when Mr. Cosgrove was presented to her. Althea was pleased to see that Noel eyed them with displeasure.

Althea did not know what she expected of the evening, but after she had spoken to a great many people she knew, and found a gaming table where the stakes were not too high to enjoy the game, she was conscious of disappointment. Dorcas had, of course, caused no scene, Lady Fabyan had not screeched anathema at Althea for encouraging Noel, and Mr. Cosgrove had not called Noel out.

The only bright spot in her evening was when she realized Dorcas was not a mewling, whining, deserted female. She spoke to Noel infrequently, apparently without rancor, and always with the same grace she might use to any man with whom she was not well acquainted.

On one level, Althea enjoyed the evening. Always smiling when in company, she moved through the evening appearing to be her usual self. But on another level, her astonished mind wondered about Dorcas and

Claude. She had not missed the gleam of interest in his eye when he was presented to the slender girl with the guinea-gold curls.

Could an alliance be possible there? Would the disappointed lovers find romance in each other? Such a tangle she had not seen since the last Minerva novel she had read.

In the novel, of course, there would be, after dire deeds and monstrous obstacles, a happy ending. Althea could not foresee in this case a happy ending, preceded as it must be by difficulties, high Cheltenham tragedies, and unhappiness.

She did not realize how much she was counting on young Noel's family, and his fiancée's family, and on Claude Cosgrove himself to straighten out the tangle. Lucy was beyond the reach of any instruction of Althea's.

At one point, she overheard a snatch of a conversation that she paid no heed to until she heard her family name.

"The young Rackham girl—" the sharp anonymous voice said, only to be hushed quickly by her companion. Sharp-voice continued in a lower tone. "Her looks must come from the Rackhams. Her mother's family was plain as ditchwater."

The other said, "I can't see her settling for an estate in Ireland, no matter how high the expectations. There's a good bit of blunt there—"

The voice was lost in the crowd then, and Althea heard no more. She was glad Mr. Cosgrove had not been within hearing.

She moved through the evening, and at last it was over. She was the richer by a little more than a guinea. On her way to find Mr. Cosgrove, she ran into Isobel Morton.

"I did not see you before," said that lady. She glanced around. "Don't tell me you have come without the delectable Miss Lucy?"

"My niece did not feel well," lied Althea promptly.

Carrying the attack forward, she added, "I hope you have won tonight?"

Sourly, Isobel said, "Of course. So, Miss Lucy Rackham does not feel well," persisted Isobel, bent on discomfiting Althea. "I suspect she is having trouble with her back."

Mystified, Althea echoed, "Her back?"

"Of course, my dear. The places where you attached your strings must be most painful." Isobel eyed her with malicious satisfaction. "Especially when you pull so desperately on them. Like a Punch-and-Judy man, but of course Lucy is no puppet. You always did like pulling strings."

"Really, Isobel, I must assure you have gone too many times to the punch bowl. I do not understand in the least what you mean."

"Don't tell me you didn't manipulate Lord Soames into using his influence about that little escapade of your niece and Lord Fabyan. I could see how you placed him in such an embarrassing situation, constraining him to come to me and beg me not to repeat the story."

"I did that?"

"Don't try to deny it. Only because I saw how miserable he was, his pride dragging in the dust, to have to do your bidding. I shall not easily forget what you have done to him."

Isobel moved on, her venom exhausted for the moment. Claude touched Althea's arm, and said, "She is a vicious woman. I trust you believe nothing of what she says."

"No, of course not." But even to her own ears she did not sound convincing.

After they had arrived in Grosvenor Square, Claude escorted her to the door. Reverting to the former topic, he said, "Of course you do not pull strings. Nobody can make anybody fall in love." The door opened and Tyson stood with the light at his back. "Nor," added Claude in an altered voice, "fall out of love."

Suddenly suspecting he had said something of importance to her, she pulled at his sleeve. "Do come in, Mr. Cosgrove. Tyson, pray bring refreshments."

The butler, looking troubled, merely bowed. Nothing could have been more proper: he held open the salon door, in which room a small fire burned brightly, and in only a few moments, he returned with a tray on which were brandy and whiskey. She felt, however, that Tyson carried a burden he wished to share with her. As she passed him, she murmured, "Later, Tyson."

When she and Mr. Cosgrove were settled and Tyson had bowed himself out, Claude said, "After all, all this talk about contracts is not to the point. Certainly I considered myself formally betrothed to Miss Lucy. And apparently Lord Fabyan and Miss More's betrothal was accomplished?"

"Published in the *Gazette*."

"Well, then, there you are."

Where? wondered Althea, but she did not need to ask. Mr. Cosgrove apparently had been accumulating a number of things to say, and presented with an opportunity, he proceeded.

"We Irish have a different outlook perhaps. A contract is but a scrap of paper, after all. It has no value unless people believe it has."

"I don't think I follow your meaning."

"A contract made by man can be broken by man."

"But everything was settled! What would happen to us all if we simply cast aside marriage contracts, and deeds, and leases, and the rest?"

"Marriage was not quite what I meant, Miss Rackham. Nobody in this unfortunate business is married. But a betrothal contract, especially one made when the principals were children, cannot have any validity unless the feelings are there."

Althea made a sound that, unkindly, sounded like a ladylike snort. "If you but knew how many arrangements were made in just such a fashion—and carried out. And none of them the worse for it."

"Are you sure? Pray forgive me if I speak of something painful to you, but your own betrothal—"

She interrupted swiftly. "That was broken, indeed, but by mutual consent." Too late she saw the pit yawning before her. Humbly she said, "Of course. I cannot insist that Lucy honor her betrothal to you when I have set such an example myself."

After a bit, she asked, "You spoke of feelings. Your own toward marrying Lucy have altered?"

Slowly he shook his head. "I realize that she is a great beauty, and that may lead her into indiscretions. She has a good intelligence, too."

Althea wondered, but did not ask, how he had arrived at that conclusion, when the girl had struck Althea as being somewhat, but not greatly, above the level of the proverbial village idiot.

"But there is something else that bothers me," he continued, "what really troubles me, Miss Rackham, is this. She is afraid of something, but what is it she is afraid of?"

With the unanswerable question ringing in her ears, she thanked him for escorting her to Lady Barnett's and watched the door close behind him.

She had gone out to be diverted, she thought ruefully, and now she was in a worse state of mind than before!

15

Tyson waited in the hall until Mr. Cosgrove was gone. Clearly he had something on his mind, and Althea preceded him into the salon again to wait, with barely concealed impatience, for him to unburden himself. She was weary and longed for her bed.

"Lord Soames called while you were out this evening," said Tyson.

"Indeed?"

"He asked for you, miss."

Then, thought Althea with satisfaction, he had not escorted Isobel to Lady Barnett's.

Tyson waited. There was more to come. "Miss Lucy received him."

Thoughtfully, Althea looked at Tyson, waiting for him to continue. But the butler had finished. At length, she murmured, "Thank you, Tyson. Good night."

She grasped the railing and pulled herself up the stairs. There was so much to think about. Isobel indicated that Simon had effectively silenced her on the matter of Noel and Lucy in the garden. That explained why no scandal had erupted on that head. She was sorry she had missed Simon tonight. She would much rather have fenced with him than won a guinea at Lady Barnett's.

Her sitting room waited in her mind's eye like a haven seen by a storm-tossed sailor. She had had her suite redecorated when she first moved here, shortly after her break with Simon. Contracts can indeed be broken, came Mr. Cosgrove's voice echoing in her mind. She had chosen cream and old rose for the room, a combination of colors that until now she had found soothing for her turbulent thoughts. Perhaps she would find the same influence tonight.

Certainly she was in need of soothing. A trying evening, considering it as a whole—Isobel's waspishness, Mr. Cosgrove's measured but unenthusiastic analysis of Lucy. He was within a breath of throwing her over, and then what would Lucy do? The match, if such could be arranged, between her and Noel Fabyan was beset by so many complications it dizzied the mind to think of it.

She reached her sitting room, grateful at least for the haven within. It was not so tonight.

She closed the door behind her. What little light there was came from a small lamp on a side table and the low, flickering fire.

Where was Pinkham? She should have seen to the fire as soon as Althea had returned home. She should have lit several lamps. Althea liked to come home to a well-lit house, and her servants knew well what was required of them.

"Pinkham?"

"I sent Pinkham away."

Startled, Althea whirled. The voice had come from the figure huddled in a chair before the dying fire, wrapped like a cocoon in an eiderdown. "Bennie! What are you doing here? Are you ill?"

Bennie looked up at her, her face drawn and white, the very image of misery. "I confess I am weary, my dear. But perhaps I am muddled only because I was asleep, very soundly, when Pinkham came. I did not know quite how to go on. But—"

Althea held up her hand. "Wait, Bennie. Is Pinkham all right?"

"Of course she is."

"Then why did she not build up the fire? I know, you said you sent her away."

"The fire was all right then."

Something had clearly happened to send her household up into the boughs. Tyson, in a voice fraught with significance, telling her that Lord Soames had called, and now Pinkham routing Bennie out of bed.

None of it made much sense to Althea. Regarding the fire critically, she realized that Bennie must have been sitting beside it for some time. And Pinkham must have lost her wits if she woke Bennie up simply for the purpose of sitting here by a dying fire.

Since it was unlikely that her maid had suddenly become a candidate for Bedlam, Althea began to realize that her house had been the scene of more than ordinary disruption. Whatever had happened, Althea did not want to hear about it, at least until she had enjoyed a night's sleep. She could scarcely keep awake now.

"Althea, I dislike very much—"

"Bennie, I am sure, when all is told, I shall dislike it too. But in the meantime, there is little advantage in sitting in a chilly room," she said briskly. "Now, not another word until I build up the fire."

She prodded the fire into renewed life. She put a block of wood on it and then, suspecting that Bennie's tale would not be quickly told, added another.

"I have some brandy here," she said. "I think we shall both be the better for it."

Not until they were settled cozily, knee to knee, the brandy warming in the glasses in their hands, did she say, "Bennie, I am so sorry that Pinkham woke you. Could she not deal with—whatever it was?"

"No, my dear, she couldn't. And I did not quite like to allow you to hear the story from her." She grimaced. "So often she exaggerates, you know."

"I know very well. Bennie, you must tell me whatever happened, at once, please. I do not enjoy hanging in suspense."

As extracted bit by bit from Bennie, whose physical weakness from her recent illness made her susceptible to fits of weeping, the story was simple enough. However, it was alarming—not so much in itself, but in what it portended.

Simply put, Pinkham had come up to Bennie's room to inform her that young miss was carrying on in a way that she, Pinkham, was not used to in Miss Rackham's house, and she, again Pinkham, would be hard put to it to think what Miss Rackham would say when she found out.

"Found out what?" demanded Althea, irritated.

That, according to Pinkham, was young miss entertaining a top-of-the-trees Corinthian, and he ought to know better being a great lord as he was in the salon with the door closed right in Tyson's face nearly taking his nose, and somebody did ought to know about it.

Bennie had an unconscious flair for mimicry. Althea could almost hear Pinkham's breathless and highly moral voice setting Miss Benbow straight, without regard for her comfort. "Right is right," as Pinkham had said, "and wrong is wrong, and young miss knows the difference or if she doesn't it's high time she did."

Bennie had then pulled herself out of her warm, comfortable bed, dressed in a hurry. "I can tell you, Althea, I do not know what I looked like, such a ramshackle job of dressing I did. But needs must, you know."

Bennie had hurried downstairs to the drawing room, whose door was no longer closed, in time to serve Lucy as chaperone. "And just in time too," added Bennie darkly.

Althea had an instant vision of Lucy swept up in Simon's arms, twisting her head frantically to avoid the rain of kisses that were falling on her face—

Unless, she thought hollowly, she had not resisted.

Tyson had seen much, if not all, of what transpired in the drawing room. Who had opened the door? Althea would never in the world ask him. "Just in time?" she asked, her tone commendably mild. "Bennie, tell me!"

Bennie did not at once answer. Althea, her suspicions ranging unchecked added, "Do you think Lucy had made an assignation with him here? Is that why she stayed home?"

Much depended on Bennie's answer. If Simon had, against all reason, conceived a passion for Lucy—who was not in the least docile, as she would take occasion to inform him at the first opportunity—and was clearly not bound by a regard for civilized behavior in his pursuit of her, Althea knew her life would be shattered. Where she had thought her days bleak before with Simon gone, she now realized that "bleak" had no meaning until now. Such behavior was not possible in the Simon she knew.

Not that she still cherished a *tendre* for him, not in the least, she told herself stoutly. The fluttering in her stomach, the blood pounding in her head, the exquisite tingling along her skin when he touched her even by the merest chance—all were simply symptoms of an unaccountable dyspepsia.

How could she have been so mistaken in anyone as depraved as Simon Halleck? She reined in her imagination sharply. "He asked for me," she said. "Do you think that was a subterfuge? That his real aim was to see Lucy?"

Bennie, even though unaware of Althea's turmoil, applied balm. "No, I truly don't think so. Indeed, Lord Soames looked vastly relieved to see me. He was most cordial."

Nearly fainting with relief, Althea managed to say, "I wager young miss, as Pinkham persists in calling her, was not best pleased."

An impish smile touched Bennie's features. "She did look most unhappy," she agreed. "I do not know what move she planned next to make, but I believe I arrived in time to forestall an incident that no one could approve."

"I do not in the least doubt you. But let us be grateful," she added, hoping for reassurance, "that Lord Soames is indeed a gentleman."

"Indeed we can," Bennie said firmly. Suddenly she laughed shakily. "I had not intended to tell you this, but I truly must. Lord Soames, always so elegant, so poised—Lord Soames was all but backed into a corner, with Lucy very close to him and looking up at him in such a way!"

They were both merry for a bit. Then, Althea looked closely at her dearest friend and did not like what she saw. "We came back too soon from Bath, I am persuaded," she told her. "I should have told Tom we could not take Lucy until you were quite well."

"Nonsense, my dear," Bennie protested. "You know it was my dearest wish to welcome Lucy."

Nonetheless, she did not demur when Althea rang for Pinkham. "We shall get you to bed at once. With a hot brick and a warm drink. And you will not get up until noon tomorrow."

Pinkham appeared suspiciously promptly, as though she had been listening outside the door. Sending her to the kitchen for brick and drink, Althea took Bennie to her room. "Lean on me, Bennie. I lean so much on you, it is only fair. I do not know what would have happened if you had not been able to chaperone Lucy."

With a quiet chuckle, Bennie objected. "I do think, you know, that I was chaperone to Lord Soames!"

After Bennie was snugly in bed, Althea dismissed Pinkham. "I can certainly undress myself. It's late and you'll be good for nothing tomorrow unless you get some sleep." When the maid reached the door, Althea spoke again. "Pinkham, you did well."

A flush of pleasure passed over Pinkham's face. "Thank you, miss," she said, and was gone.

Althea drew a chair up near Bennie's bed. "I shall stay till you fall asleep. I know you will tell me there is no need for that, but I am not in the least sleepy. This incident has driven any weariness right out of me."

"Lucy does have a tendency to unsettle people, does

she not? I have never seen a more beautiful young lady. She must have inherited her looks from her mother. But I do confess to being just a little disappointed in her mind."

Althea agreed dryly. "Rather a common mind, wouldn't you say? That, too, she must have inherited from her mother." Something caught at her mind then, something that she thought she should remember and consider. Rather like a thorn catching at one's skirt when picking blackberries in the country. But she could not just now remember what it was.

Althea deliberately put Simon out of her thoughts. Bennie had rescued the situation, and Simon, delighted with her intervention, had made a swift departure. Lucy had gone upstairs in fuming silence, refusing to listen to Bennie, and in fact closing the door firmly between them.

Since she had banished Simon for the night, her thoughts turned again to the evening just past, without pleasure. Was she indeed a puppetmaster, as Isobel had accused her? Or would it be puppetmistress? The core of the matter was, was she in fact using Lucy for her own ends?

Earlier, without doubt, she had prodded Simon into anger over her own refusal to commit herself to preventing any marriage between Lucy and Noel. Examining her actions seriously, in the bright light directed thereto by Isobel Morton, she realized that there was blame to be assigned, and she bore the brunt of it.

She herself wished devoutly that Lucy would forget Noel Fabyan. If she wished to marry Mr. Cosgrove or did not directly concern Althea. But as long as Simon thought that Noel was in danger of contracting a mesalliance with Lucy, he was bound to keep an eye on the situation. A close eye, Althea hoped.

Althea considered the potential match as much a mesalliance as Simon did. But she had indicated to him that she would favor such a marriage. Only, she reminded herself, *only* for the purpose of bringing Simon back to her.

Puppet strings!

In an agony of self-abasement she examined her motives for enticing Simon to return. She had previously convinced herself that under no circumstances would she rekindle feelings she had long since extinguished. Love could be stifled, but never totally extinguished. She knew it would take very little to revive the corpse.

Suddenly Bennie stirred. "You are not at all sleepy, are you?"

"I am not, but I cannot conceive why you should not be. The warmth of your bed must be most comfortable."

"It is, but I think the brandy makes me wakeful. I am not used to it at bedtime, you know."

She sat up in bed, losing a corner of the eiderdown. Pulling it again around her shoulders, she asked, "How was your evening?"

Althea did not answer directly. Instead, she said, "Do you think Lucy is afraid?"

"Afraid? Of what?" said Bennie, a trifle crossly. "I doubt that anyone who has seen tigers and elephants would fear anything. She certainly did not fear Lord Soames."

Diverted, Althea asked, "Tigers? Really? She has told you this?"

"She has told me nothing, even when I inquired about her life there, you know. But she lived in India. Tigers live in India." She turned thoughtful, however, and at last she said, "Afraid? You know, I wonder."

Althea had not expected confirmation of Mr. Cosgrove's suggestion. Now she leaned forward. "About what?"

"She never talks about India," said Bennie slowly. "I don't know whether she lived with tigers around her every day, or in the mountains. I have heard her talking with Molly, but she stops when I come in."

"Perhaps she doesn't want to bring up sad memories," said Althea, not believing it. "But perhaps there is something right here to fear. For instance, she may not be quite so confident as she seems to be about carrying out her plans to ensnare that foolish Lord Fabyan."

"Foolish?"

"Dorcas More has beautiful eyes and lovely gold curls. I found a sweetness in her manners that is very winning."

"Was Lord Fabyan with her tonight?"

"Indeed he was. And his mother not far away. But somehow Miss More did not give me the impression that she was pining away from lack of attention from Noel. In truth, I did wonder whether she wasn't becoming more than passably interested in Mr. Cosgrove!"

"Mr. Cosgrove? I do find that difficult to believe."

"He paid her marked attention. In fact, I was left much to myself."

She and Bennie gossiped for a bit about Lady Barnett's affair, and finally, seeing that Bennie was at last becoming drowsy, Althea said, "I think we'll both sleep now." She pressed Bennie back on the pillows and tucked the eiderdown around her shoulders.

"What are you going to do about her?" asked Bennie, already half-asleep.

"I haven't decided yet. I just don't know."

Back in her room, Althea undressed herself and climbed into bed. She was nearly as sleepy now as she had been when she had seen Mr. Cosgrove out, even though much of a stimulating nature had occurred in the interval.

Phrases came back to haunt her: puppet on a string . . . contract made can be broken . . . what will you do next? And her own answer, I just don't know.

In dealing with such a headstrong young lady, what *could* she do?

16

In the end, Althea did nothing.

Lucy seemed to have learned something from the unfortunate incident of that night. For the first day or two she eyed Althea much as a young colt might watch its master arriving with bridle in hand. Althea made no reference to Lucy's indelicate behavior, and gradually Lucy lost her apprehension, and life at the Grosvenor Square house returned to normal.

At least, thought Althea, to what passes for normal these days. She reflected that her disposition was well on its way to turning to vinegar, and she would be well out of it if she did not in the end run Miss Jenny a close second for malicious pessimism.

Now that Lucy had been presented to society, invitations poured in. Her glossy black hair and huge violet eyes were assets that attracted suitors as a magnet attracts filings.

It was captious, Althea told herself, to be the slightest bit critical of Lucy's conversation. As long as the girl beamed impartially upon everyone, she was a delight. But prolonged exposure to her conversation, self-centered as it was, might well result in a wish for a blander diet. And in truth, while the numbers of suitors attracted to her remained fairly constant, Althea noticed that the faces changed.

Mr. Cosgrove, nonetheless, remained faithful.

However, it did not take long for Althea, noting the constant restlessness of Lucy's eyes, as though searching for someone not at hand, to realize that Noel Fabyan had not appeared, either at the many private parties where he could have been expected, or calling in Grosvenor Square.

Althea should have felt much easier in her mind. It seemed obvious that Lord Soames had exercised his powerful influence on his nephew and made such strong representations to the young man on the subject of his duty to his family that, even infatuated as Noel was, he feared to defy him.

Lady Fabyan, of course, was also in town. Althea had felt the sharp edge of her tongue and did not relish it. How much more cutting would she be in dealing with her son than she had been with Althea, a comparative stranger?

Noel's defection was beginning to tell on Lucy, whose mood in public became erratic and at home was downright morose. Only the prospect of a theater party was able to bring her out of her depression.

But typically Lucy sought to turn even her failings into advantages. Knowing that her aunt was aware of her unhappiness, and conceiving that Althea must be worried about her, she said, in a die-away manner that she had just perfected, "I do not know whether I shall wish to go."

"You must make up your mind, Lucy," said Althea calmly. "Sir Horace Wychley is most generous to invite us, and he must not be left dangling. I am sure you will find the affair delightful."

"Perhaps," she sighed, "but if I go I shall wear my saffron gown. I have not worn it yet."

Althea was well aware of that. She had not allowed Lucy to wear it at her reception, since it was cut quite low, but Lucy had been out for some time now, and Althea judged it wise to ease the restrictions placed on her.

"Very well," she said. "See that Molly has it well pressed. I do not think the pearls are suitable. Let me think what will go best."

The theater party was all that Lucy hoped for. She wore her saffron gown, with a simple choker of amber beads furnished by her aunt. The play, which she did not understand, was no distraction for her, so she could enjoy to the fullest the attentions that came her way.

Mr. Cosgrove was not one of the party, but he called on them at their box during the intermission.

"I wonder at you, Mr. Cosgrove," said Lucy, "that you could leave Miss More for the evening. I am told you are quite gallant with your attentions to her."

"I see her," he said unchivalrously, "no oftener than I see any other lady of my acquaintance."

"Even so," said Noel Fabyan, joining them in time to overhear the conversation, "you call quite too frequently."

Lucy stiffened. He was entirely too partial to his fiancée to suit her.

Immediately conscious of his gaffe, he blundered on, "Her aunt doesn't like it above half!"

Mr. Cosgrove bowed formally, his cheeks reddening. "Perhaps Lady Barnett would do me the honor of telling me so, in that event."

The two young men faced each other like cockerels, Althea thought, and unless she was mistaken, there were the makings of a very fine quarrel here, in public, and in all likelihood even Simon could not prevent the tale from running like wildfire. There were too many witnesses.

Fortunately, one of the witnesses was Simon. She noticed thankfully his tall figure on the fringe of the persons, mostly male, clustered around Lucy. Her relief must have appeared in her face, for he smiled slightly. His eyes, though, were warm with amusement. She felt more in charity with him at that moment than for years.

As one by one Noel, Mr. Cosgrove, and the others became aware of Simon's quiet presence, they fell silent. He spoke to Lucy, but his eyes, conveying a message, were fixed on Althea.

"I have come, Miss Lucy, to beg of you a favor. I have long wanted to entertain you in Berkeley Square."

"H-how very nice!" breathed Lucy.

"I have presumed greatly, I know, but I have hopes that you—and the rest of Sir Horace's party, of course —would join me after the theater? A modest collation, nothing pretentious. May I hope for your acceptance?"

"Oh, Aunt, I should like it above all things! Do say we may!"

Mindful of the message sent to her by Simon's significant glance, even though she did not quite understand what he wanted of her, Althea accepted for them all, and the details were settled in a moment.

Lucy ignored the last act of the play entirely. Althea stole a sidelong glance at her from time to time, surprising her in a secret smile. It was clear to Althea that Lucy believed Simon's invitation was entirely for her. Good God, did she think that she had made an overwhelming impression on him the other night at Grosvenor Square?

An even more lowering thought came to her then. Did Lucy expect to capture Simon's hand, if not his heart? Such a catch would be a spectacular coup, considering that he had once expected to marry her aunt, and rumor tied him to Isobel Morton and half a dozen others whose qualifications were formidable. Surely Lucy must have at least a modicum of Rackham sense!

Althea was confirmed in her doubts when Lucy, under cover of the final music of the play, leaned toward her and said, "Are you sure, Aunt Althea, that you wish to go on to Lord Soames'? I do not think you look quite well."

Looking steadily at Lucy, she said clearly, "I am quite well, thank you. Your concern is especially touching when you must realize that if I am to return home at once, I shall require you to accompany me."

Lucy glared defiantly at her, but it was the younger woman who was first to turn away. Nursing an unworthy feeling of triumph, Althea followed Lucy down the stairs, into Sir Horace's carriage, and they set out in the wake of Simon's carriage for Berkeley Square.

Lucy would have to be forgiven if she received the impression that Lord Soames was endeavoring particularly to please her. The collation, which he had termed modest, was by any standard sumptuous. The Prince Regent himself, a notable connoisseur, would have approved.

Noel and Mr. Cosgrove disapproved of Simon's arrangement, each in his own way and for his own reasons. Noel had no need to envy his uncle's wealth, but he could, and did, speak to the point on a subject that chafed him.

He drew Simon aside and addressed him in a voice that he did not take the trouble to lower. "Turning the lady's head, Uncle, not quite the best form, is it?"

His uncle surveyed him briefly and coolly. "I think you have been too often to the punch bowl, Noel. Pray mend your manners."

"Manners, is it? Pretty manners from a man old enough to be her father. I don't suppose that occurred to you? Not the thing to call you out, being related, but damned if I don't think I will!"

Something in his uncle's icy eye suddenly sobered him. He flushed momentarily and mumbled a phrase that Simon, full of charity, chose to regard as an apology. "Get some food in your stomach, Noel," he advised in a low voice. With a gesture he summoned a footman, and Noel was soon provided with solid refreshment.

Althea, desirous of ferreting out Simon's design in this uncalled-for midnight supper, had watched the entire scene between Noel and his uncle. This sottish behavior on the part of Noel Fabyan might well put an end to Lucy's infatuation with him, but on the other hand, Simon's elegance and effortless authority in dealing with Noel could not fail to make an impression on the girl.

Mr. Cosgrove, too, had watched with interest, but without a word. Instead, he had engaged Lucy in conversation in a vain attempt to prevent her from seeing the unedifying spectacle. Lucy, however, had eyes only for Simon.

Sir Horace sat next to Althea at supper. He leaned toward her. "This is a rum go, Althea."

"I couldn't agree more."

"I suppose we can't leave now, but I swear I wish this business was done with."

"As soon as we can," Althea promised, "we shall depart."

Supper passed, eventually, as conversation languished, and Althea was wrapped in her own thoughts. Mr. Cosgrove, as befitted a country gentleman, made steady inroads on the food provided, but Noel pushed his around on the plate. Clearly everyone else had lost interest in the evening, save for Lucy, who had embarked on a program of sighs and fluttering eyelashes, sweet smiles, and adoring looks, all of which Simon appeared to take as only his due.

When they rose from supper, Althea drew him aside. Clutching his sleeve, she whispered fiercely, "Have you taken leave of your senses? What game are you playing here?"

Simon's grin was wicked. "Pray don't tell me you are jealous, for I shan't believe you."

"Jealous! Never in the world! How vain you are, Simon, to think that I would be." She regarded him through narrowed eyelids. In a cool voice, she said, "A red herring, I fancy. Do stick to the point, Simon. You must realize you are turning the girl's head?"

"The girl's head is on a swivel," he said. "Like a weathercock. Now Noel, now me, next Mr. Cosgrove—"

"Oh, no," she burst out. "Never Mr. Cosgrove."

Interested, he inquired, "How do you know that?"

Too late, she remembered the precise conversation that had impressed itself on her mind. There was nothing for it but to confide in Simon. Old habits are hard to break, she thought. "No Mrs. Anybody," she said.

"But Lady Anybody?" he guessed. "Such a wretched girl. This is a trial that I should not have expected even Tom to subject you to."

His gaze was warm, and for a moment she felt the old magic he could always work. For that moment, she was again loved, tenderly cared for, wrapped in the security of his regard.

"Althea—" he began in an altered tone.

While Simon and Althea were talking, Noel, plagued both by a guilty conscience over Dorcas and an intensely sharp jealousy over Lucy, had recourse again to an unattended decanter of whiskey. He drank off his first glass quickly and poured another.

His uncle would not approve, he thought, but he decided he did not care. His uncle might be twice the man Noel was—as Noel admitted only when he was truly foxed—but Noel Fabyan was head of his family and it was beyond anything that Simon dared to interfere with Fabyan affairs.

It was Lucy's ill luck that, returning from a small parlor put at the disposal of female guests, she met Noel in the hall.

"S-so," Noel said, swaying before her and barring her passage, "you think you're going to haul in Uncle Simon at the end of your line? Believe me, you—you're using the wrong b-bait. He's not one for ninny-hammers."

Lucy was inexperienced in the world of London society, but she was not totally without sense. She could recognize a drunken man when she saw him, and she certainly was faced with one at this moment. Lest there be any doubt about it, she said with disgust, "You're drunk! Let me pass!"

"S-so I am," agreed Noel, nodding sagely and continuously like a mandarin.

Whether it was simply a matter of losing his balance and reaching out for support, or whether his intention was more sinister, would never be known. The result, however, had all the impact of fireworks in the sky.

Noel stumbled, lurched, grabbed. Lucy, feeling his heavy hands on her shoulders, screamed faintly. She saw all her dreams of becoming Somebody, her long weeks of tightly controlled scheming, doing the right thing according to Miss Benbow and Aunt Althea, the dedicated ambition the existence of which she believed she had carefully hidden from everyone—all falling disastrously to the ground like a house of cards scattered by a careless, impersonal hand.

Much, she thought as she staggered a few steps backward under the impetus of Noel's body, as she was now falling physically to the polished floor of Lord Soames' fashionable Berkeley Square house.

Seeing her plans demolished and fearing that of it all she might not preserve even her virginity, to say nothing of her dignity, she opened her mouth to scream with purpose. Although her initial screams were worthy of attention, even more volume was added as she heard a long ripping sound, as the delicate fabric of her favorite and vastly becoming saffron gown gave way.

The sound of the impact as the two bodies, one alcoholicly inert and the other struggling feverishly, hit the floor vibrated throughout the ground floor, gathering an instantaneous audience.

When the sound of scuffling from the hall reached Simon and Althea, they hesitated, listening. Then

Lucy's penetrating scream rose into the air, the first of a series, and Simon, mumbling a curse at the interruption, was through the door in two strides. Althea was on his heels, so closely that when he stopped abruptly, she ran into him.

The sight that met the appalled gaze of those assembled was so grotesque as to defy immediate analysis. All Althea could be certain of was that all previous social contretemps, even scandal and disaster, were as nothing compared to this—this *catastrophe.*

"Good God, Noel! What are you doing?" Simon roared. Then, realizing that he had phrased the question poorly under the circumstances, he stopped short. A stifled gasp from behind caused him to turn. "Althea, my dear," he exclaimed, "it is not what you think! It cannot be!"

Her lips moved, but she made no sound. It was Lucy on the floor. She could see the fabric of the saffron skirt, partly hidden from view by a pair of black trousered legs. L-Lucy—assaulted? Simon's arms went around her, comforting, protecting. With one hand he turned her head away from the scene on the floor.

By this time, Mr. Cosgrove had taken charge. He reached down to grab Noel's collar and without hesitation pulled strongly upward. So might one remove a dog forcibly from a fight.

On his feet, Noel swayed still, but it was clear that he was much sobered by the incident. Indeed, as he looked down at Lucy, moaning yet, he paled to a greenish-white hue and covered his face with his hands. "Oh, God, what have I done?"

He might well ask, thought Althea frantically as she thrust Simon aside, placed her hand in the middle of Noel's chest and pushed him away, and dropped to her knees beside Lucy.

"My dear girl," Althea crooned, "where does it hurt? Can you move your limbs?"

Automatically she tugged the saffron skirt into a

more seemly position. She smoothed the dark curls away from Lucy's brow. Lucy opened her eyes abruptly and stared wildly around her. Seeing Lucy's mouth opening, Althea placed her palm firmly over it to stifle the inevitable scream. "Now, Lucy," she said in a brisker manner, "I note you are able to move without difficulty. I wish you to get up, so I may see how badly you are injured."

"My dress," cried Lucy. "My dress is ruined!" With Mr. Cosgrove's strong hand under her arm, Lucy struggled to her feet.

The gown was, Althea believed, not irretrievably damaged. "Miss Hope will mend it," she said. She placed her own shawl around Lucy's bare shoulders. Noel's hand had caught, when he clawed for his balance, in the neckline of her frock, and in falling had ripped the bodice all the way to her waist.

Sir Horace belatedly became aware of an unusual flurry behind him. He had never admitted to himself what his many friends could have told him: he was growing more than a little deaf.

Therefore, he had no clear idea of the magnitude of the upheaval in the inner hall. He sauntered to the connecting door and peered through. The sight that met his eyes struck him speechless.

Mr. Cosgrove was squared off in fighting stance, his fist quivering directly before Noel's nose. Noel, however, was putting up no kind of resistance. Indeed, young Lord Fabyan looked more than a little drunk, his expression woebegone, even appalled, but not catching anyone's eye.

Lord Soames looked grim as death and leaned against the door frame, a crease between his eyebrows, brooding on the scene.

And Althea—her arm around Lucy, talking soothingly to her, turning her gently away from Noel. And Lucy—by gum! the girl's frock in rags!

Sir Horace was not blessed with imagination. Even so, it took little effort for him to realize that something

out of the ordinary had just taken place. Young
Fabyan's father was a loose screw. It looked like young
Noel was cut from the same cloth. But a young lady,
and in his uncle's house? The boy was overdue at
Bedlam!

The whole thing was queer as Dick's hatband. Even
Soames couldn't keep this business under cover. Sir
Horace was aware of an unworthy wish that he had
insisted on going home after the theater.

To his credit was the fact that such a wish lasted
only a moment, and was indeed directed more toward
the welfare of the ladies in his charge than to himself.

Althea's voice was asking the same question that Sir
Horace would like to have answered. "What happened,
Lucy? Can you tell us?"

Lucy wrapped the shawl tightly around her and held
it fast over her bosom. She took a long shuddering
breath, which calmed her. "I am not hurt at all, Aunt."
She turned deliberately to face Noel. "It was only that
Lord Fabyan lost his balance, and I fear I was not
strong enough to sustain him."

Sir Horace had been holding his breath for the
answer. He let it out in an explosive puff. "Good!
Thought for a moment—"

Mr. Cosgrove said heavily, "We all thought, Sir
Horace." He looked at Lucy with an unreadable expression and relaxed his belligerent posture. "But it
seems we were mistaken."

With Lucy's explanation, it was as though they had
all returned to life. The visitors stirred themselves in
the direction of the entry, and Noel, mumbling dis-
jointed words of apology, followed them.

Simon had not lost his grimness, but it was confined
now to his eyes. He managed a civil smile to speed his
guests on their way. He held Althea's hand a trifle
longer than was strictly necessary. "I cannot tell you
how deeply I regret this business."

She gave him a tremulous smile and withdrew her

hand. "It seems that no harm was done. I am prepared to put the evening out of my mind."

"All of it?"

She knew he referred to that moment before Lucy's scream, the moment in which she thought they were moving together toward an agreement both portentous and delightful.

"Not all of it," she murmured.

There was time in the coach on the way home to examine that scene in the hall, the scene which in her most vivid imagination Althea could not have expected to take place.

The more she thought of it, the less satisfied she was with Lucy's explanation. Noel was indeed drunk. The question was, was he merely sufficiently foxed to fall, as Lucy explained, reaching out frantically for support, or was he even drunker, enough to forget every scruple of a gentleman and make an attempt upon a young lady of quality?

She tried to remember the exact expression on Noel's face. Was it shame at being drunk in company, or did he remember what he had attempted? There had been a surprising gleam in Noel's eye, passing in a moment, when Lucy had exonerated him from base intentions. She wished she could know what flashed through his mind at that time.

In the carriage, she asked a tentatively probing question. "Do you suppose Noel will remember just what happened when he returns to himself in the morning?"

Lucy's answer was unsatisfactory. "He will remember."

The tone in which she spoke indicated—at least to Althea, who was losing some of the illusions she had first entertained about Lucy—that if Noel did not recall the event, she was more than willing to remind him.

Lucy thanked Sir Horace prettily and, after entering the house, hurried up to her bedchamber, pleading exhaustion. As well she might, thought Althea.

Once Althea was in the quiet peace of her sitting room, with only Pinkham on hand to undress her, she began to feel the delayed effects of the unpleasant ending of her evening.

Fortunately Bennie was safely asleep. Althea would have to concoct a tale to tell her, for the truth was bound to overset her. Bennie was in sad need of a rest, or another visit to the restorative waters of Bath, but until Lucy was elsewhere, was married or at the least placed in Caroline's hands at Darley Hall, Bennie would not budge from Grosvenor Square.

Poor Bennie—taking on this child as the only tangible remembrance she had of the man she had loved! Althea realized that she had not shared many of the small irritations that Lucy strewed in her wake. And certainly she did not wish to tell Bennie about Noel's fall, or his attempted assault, whichever it was.

Pinkham suspected that something was amiss. "I daresay that young miss," she probed, "is having trouble making up her mind?"

"About what?"

"Whether to cut you out with Lord Soames."

"Pinky, you overstep. Miss Lucy is entirely too young to think of marrying yet. And it is no secret in this house that she is promised to Mr. Cosgrove."

"He don't seem to care much about it, I've noticed. No, mark my words, she's got her cap set for bigger fish."

"Pinky, that's ridiculous. She is only eighteen, you know."

"Aye, I know, so she says."

"Pinky, that is enough. And if I hear that you are talking in this fashion to the rest of the household, I shall make you regret it."

She had hurt Pinkham, she knew, but she needed to

be alone. She suffered through another few moments of her maid's services, before she said, "Goodness, don't fuss so. I can get into my robe by myself." In a kinder voice, she said, "Go to bed, Pinky. It's very late." Pinkham was mollified.

Left to herself, Althea knew she would not sleep for hours. Too much wine at supper, too much turmoil later. Pinkham's remarks did not comfort. She was too tired to think profitably, she knew that. But nonetheless small recollections—not only of this evening, but of other incidents—swam through her mind like a school of fish. There was one fish she knew had some meaning for her, if she could only catch it. Someone, somewhere, had said something that she overheard, that she should remember. She had almost caught its significance at the time, and at odd moments since had wondered about what it was, and what it meant—some fact or opinion?

It was no use. She could never recall it by trying so hard. Instead, she might well try to puzzle out the truth of the affair tonight. Lucy said Noel had fallen, but the root of Althea's disbelief lay in the odd note in Lucy's voice when she explained what had happened. Yet, Althea and Simon were immediately on the scene, and as Althea closed her eyes and brought the scene to life in her mind, there was nothing—not a word, not an unexplained state of clothing, or position of body, nothing—to support a charge of attempted assault.

Lucy, she was sure now, told the truth. Why, then, did she make the truth sound false?

Just before Althea slipped off into sleep, she remembered the words she had been trying this long time to remember. They were spoken not by one person, but by various people.

They fell together now to make a picture in her mind. A picture of questions unanswered, a picture containing incredible suggestions and large vacant spaces. The picture grew larger in her drowsy mind. The surface of it seemed reasonable enough, but there lurked behind it a glimmer of an astounding question that she had not dreamed of asking . . .

As sleep overtook her, she knew what she must do on the morrow.

17

Althea, next morning, sent Samuel with a note to an address just off Duke Street, a house that had recently been hired for the Season by Lady St. Aubyn.

Althea had just seen her in the Pump Room at Bath, wrapped up like a mummy, her debilitated condition and unhealthily yellow complexion lending verisimilitude to the comparison.

Although Althea did not know her, she remembered that Lady St. Aubyn had claimed acquaintance with the late Lady Darley, and Althea hoped the older woman was well enough to see her. She was. Samuel returned in a very short time with a note, fixing eleven o'clock that morning.

She stepped down from her town landau onto the pavement before Lady St. Aubyn's house. She had not allowed herself time to reflect upon her decision of the night before. She was not even sure she knew what question she would ask Lady St. Aubyn, nor indeed whether she wished to hear the answer.

But that Lady St. Aubyn held a key to a part of the puzzle that was beginning to haunt Althea, she was sure. The puzzle was not a thing of slow growth, of a hint here, of an odd remark there, building a structure, as it were, all of a piece.

Indeed, Althea was not sure it was a puzzle at all. But although it had come together in her mind only the night before, it had already begun to haunt her with

unanswered, perhaps unanswerable questions. At the
center of it was Lucy. She was, on the surface, a young
miss of eighteen—"so she says," according to Pinkham—of good family but without elegant training. The
girl seemed pleasant enough and, except for some
notable exceptions, eager to learn and to move correctly in society.

Lucy baffled Althea. Nobody could live so entirely
on the surface. There must be real thoughts, real
dreams, genuine feelings behind the outer, polite
appearance she presented.

The door to Lady St. Aubyn's house opened, and
Althea went in. "My lady is expecting you, miss," said
the woman who had opened the door. Tall, angular,
dyed dark hair, a forbidding expression—she was
daunting. But when she introduced Althea into the
drawing room, she looked at her mistress with a
certain light in her eyes that spoke of doglike devotion.
Althea liked her much better.

And she liked Lady St. Aubyn at once.

"My dear Althea, how delighted I am that you wrote
to me," said her hostess in a low, musical voice that
struck pleasantly on the ear. "I would have written to
you eventually, but this is much better. Come and sit
here, where I can see you."

Althea did as she was bid, sitting in a low chair
opposite Lady St. Aubyn where the light from the
window streamed brightly in.

"Is the light too much? I am so used to it, you know,
for the light in India is quite blinding. I find rooms in
London so dark in consequence."

"I trust I see you quite well again."

"Indeed I am. It was a dreadful voyage home, you
know, storms around the Cape, and I am never a good
sailor. Besides, I was not well at the start. I must make
that my excuse."

"Excuse? I am persuaded you would never need an
excuse for anything."

"For not going out in society, you know. I still feel

not strong at times, but I am assured by the autumn I will be myself again."

"It must be tedious not to see your friends," Althea offered. She was beginning to feel a great affinity for the other woman, an immediate conviction that she could trust her, and almost—to her own astonishment —almost a feeling that if she could have chosen her own mother, she would without question have selected Lady St. Aubyn.

"Your mother," said Lady St. Aubyn, "was dear to me. I felt such loss when I heard that she had died. You were quite young then?"

"I was thirteen."

"And you've grown into a very attractive young lady. She would have been pleased. But we shall not rake over old coals. There are sufficiently unhappy occurrences to deal with, without clinging to old griefs."

"Were you long in India?" wondered Althea, obediently changing the subject.

"Long enough. India, I can tell you, is no place for women. Nor children. It is hot and dusty and full of pernicious diseases for those who are not native. As you see."

"No tigers?"

"Yes, indeed. All kinds of game. One day I shall tell you of the travels we made in that country, sometimes on camels, sometimes on elephants. An official progress, as it was called, was a spectacle so colorful, so unbelievably grand—sometimes there were as many as ten thousand persons in the caravan— But, my dear Althea, I think you did not come to hear an old woman's reminiscences?"

"Indeed I should like to hear them, and I wish my errand could be forgotten."

"Then let us deal with it now and have it done with."

Althea's hands turned in her lap. Lady St. Aubyn was much different from what she had expected. The mummified invalid of Bath had turned into a charming, shrewd, cosmopolitan noblewoman. The puzzle that had brought Althea here seemed all at once to be the stuff of dreams. Or, rather, nightmares.

This small reception room shrieked of the commonplace. The chairs and tables were those to be met with in any house Althea visited. There was no trace of brass gongs or temple bells, evocative of India, and therefore providing some tie to Lucy.

"I hardly know how to start," she confessed.

Again Lady St. Aubyn read her thoughts. "I have been wondering when you would call on me."

"But I should not have dared—"

"I suppose not, on the basis of our brief conversation at the Pump Room. But I think you have another reason?"

"I am not sure, but I think so." Then, catching a nuance in Lady St. Aubyn's words, she asked, "You expected me?"

The other woman nodded. "It was only a matter of time."

"Then, could you possibly know what is on my mind?"

The answer came slowly. "Perhaps not precisely. But I do keep up with the gossip, you know. I am blessed with many good friends and a large number of relations. Not all of them are blessings, of course, but one accepts them." She smiled wryly. "And I do know the current *on-dits.*"

Lady St. Aubyn's deep-blue eyes were steady on hers. Althea felt a sudden excitement, a suggestion that she was on the verge of discovery. But discovery of what, she had no idea.

"Where shall I start?" Althea wondered. "First, I want to say how kind it was of you to offer condolences when I met you in Bath."

"The proper thing to do. But you were surprised?"

"A trifle. Only because your sympathy was somewhat belated."

"Not at all belated. There was no opportunity to write, even though I must have sent it to Darley Hall rather than your town house. I had not heard of your legacy until I arrived in England. How fortunate for you! I should imagine, if your brother is at all like your father—and I am sure he must be, for Edward was entirely different—that you are relieved to live away from Lord Darley's family."

"The opportunity came at a most timely moment."

"Of course. It is always an advantage to live a year or two on your own before marrying."

"I have no plans to marry."

"Pray don't think me prying, my dear. I adored your mother, and I see much of her in you. I have no children of my own, and I have kept *au courant* on your affairs. But there again, that is not why you came to see me."

"Tell me about my brother, if you will. You knew him well?"

"Very well indeed. My husband thought much of him, as did I. He was a mad, brave man who could not be denied promotion, although they tried. His men worshipped him, you see, and there was nothing they wouldn't do for him. I believe it was thought that mutiny was in the wind, before he was made colonel."

"How different that is from anything I was ever told of him! He has been gone these eighteen months, but it is as though he died when I was five. That is why, I suppose, I considered your condolences belated. It was uncivil in me to say so."

"You referred to my sympathy for Edward? Gracious, no! I wrote what was proper to your brother at the time."

"But did I misunderstand? I believed you said your first opportunity—"

"My dear, we are wandering in a maze. Rather, two mazes, for we are not at all on the same road. My condolences were not for your brother."

Althea sat very still. She could hear a significance

lying beneath the words Lady St. Aubyn spoke. But she understood nothing.

"No wonder you were startled, when I spoke to you. I think perhaps we should set directly about straightening ourselves out. Colonel Rackham died eighteen months ago. You were informed of that, I am sure."

"Yes, Tom received a letter."

"And, if you will forgive me, what else was in the letter? Did it speak of anyone else?"

Althea frowned, trying to remember the details. "I do not think so. But you must know that some four months ago, Tom received word through Mr. Dedham, his attorney, that Edward was married and had a daughter. This surely is correct."

"In every detail."

"This, you must know, was the first indication we had that he had married."

"Small wonder," said Lady St. Aubyn tartly. "The woman was a fool."

"Was? We were not sure, but we supposed that she must have died long since. And my niece does not speak of her."

"You do not surprise me."

"My sister-in-law then is deceased?"

"Fifteen years since."

"That explains it, then," mused Althea. If the girl had no mother to see that she was properly reared, she could not be blamed for the failings that Althea was becoming daily more aware of.

"Forgive me, Althea, but it explains nothing. At least, nothing of the matter at hand."

Bewildered by the other's cryptic statements, which were at best vague and at worst without sense, Althea wondered how soon she could take her leave. The woman must be addled, perhaps from illness, perhaps from a long sojourn under a hot tropical sun, and Althea was sorry for her. But most of all, she was disappointed in the extreme. She had come with high hopes, with the expectation of piecing out the puzzle that quite haunted her, and she had received almost nothing of any help.

"You are disappointed, my dear," said Lady St. Aubyn, once again saying aloud Althea's own thoughts. "Pray don't be. We have much to talk about yet. I think—yes, I think we shall have a dish of tea, and then I will tell you a story."

The tea was hot and strong, marvelously restoring. When they had finished, Althea was ready to hear any story, even one about a mythical maharaja and his mythical rubies. One of Bennie's romantic novels had dealt with just such a subject.

"Shall I start?" said Lady St. Aubyn whimsically, " 'Once upon a time'? My story is not quite a fairy tale, though I promise you you will find some of it hard to believe."

"Please tell me," Althea said earnestly. "I have a great need to know about my brother Edward and—and his family."

"Any particular reason?"

"That is the trouble. I do not know, but I have a feeling—indeed, I fear that something is amiss, and yet I cannot tell why I think so."

Lady St. Aubyn nodded briskly. "I shall tell you why you think so. But first let me go back nearly twenty years. I was newly married and my husband and I sailed to India, where he was to join his regiment. Since I was young and perhaps frivolous, I grew to know my husband's officers quite intimately. One of them was Edward Rackham. We knew there was some scandal about his leaving England, and at first he was treated with reserve, but he was so charming—like your mother, Althea—and so unassuming that before long he was respected and admired. His greatest friend was Charles Cosgrove. Does that name signify anything to you?"

"Not Charles. But I am acquainted with a Claude Cosgrove, as I suspect you well know. Is there much that goes on in London that you are not informed of?"

"Very little. At any rate, Charles Cosgrove and your uncle were great friends. They fought together, spent their leaves together, planned eventually to return to Ireland to Charles' family estates together. Charles had left his wife behind, but he had no doubt she would like Edward quite as much as he did. And then Miss Ainsley came upon the scene."

"I have heard that name. Margaret Ainsley, I think?"

"Yes. Dear plain-featured, whining Margaret. To play fair, her position was unpleasant. She was distantly related to Sir Lewis Upham, the commanding general at the time, and he had sent for Margaret to wait on Lady Upham. *There* was an unpleasant woman for you. If we had been back in King James's time, she would have been burned at the stake. Not for witchcraft, which of course nobody believes in now, but for sheer malicious cruelty. No wonder Margaret snatched at straws."

"My brother Edward," said Althea wisely.

"He was not a straw, of course. But Margaret paid no heed to whether they would suit. She was a remarkably silly woman. She produced a daughter in short order, and three years later died."

"That was fifteen years ago, was it not? And we are speaking of Lucy."

Lady St. Aubyn's expression was odd. "Yes, we are speaking of Lucy. My husband, Anthony, was transferred up-country then, and I did not see either Charles Cosgrove or your uncle for some years. We had our own troubles, you know. We were quite near the Khyber, and the Pathans resented us greatly." She lapsed into memory. Finally, she shook her head sharply, as though to banish unwelcome visions. "I shall tell you about that, too, someday."

"I shall look forward to it. But what happened to Lucy?"

Lady St. Aubyn looked searchingly at her. "You really don't know, do you?"

"No, ma'am, I don't." Althea knew that the answer to the puzzle was dangling just before her eyes. In a moment she would understand. This was comforting, because at this point she did not know what there was to understand. She felt uneasy, that was all. Then she remembered a piece of the puzzle.

"Lady St. Aubyn, you said that my sister-in-law was a plain-featured woman."

"Very."

"And the Rackhams have produced not great beauties in six generations."

Lady St. Aubyn regarded her as though a favorite pupil had translated a particularly difficult passage in Aeschylus. "Go on, my dear."

"Then," said Althea slowly, working out concretely the vague ideas that had come to her from time to time, "where did Lucy's beauty, which I assure you is magnificent, come from? A by-blow?"

"Never. I assure you Margaret was painfully faithful."

"You know?"

"I do not know in the least where your Lucy's looks came from. But I tell you this. Edward's daughter, Lucy Rackham, died of the plague in Bombay five months ago."

Althea's lips moved. Plague? Died? *Died?* She realized that she had made no sound.

Lady St. Aubyn was bending over her with a small vile-smelling bottle, saying, "There, there. Just breathe. You'll be fine. I should not have told you like this."

The pungent scent from the bottle stung her nose and she turned her head away and sneezed. Her hostess must have rung for more tea, because a cup of it, fragrant and steaming, was placed in her hand. "Don't talk, Althea," said Lady St. Aubyn's voice somewhere above Althea's head. "Drink your tea and then we can consider what's to be done."

The most restoring words Althea could have heard

were the last—"what's to be done." Althea knew then that whatever happened, she had a firm friend in Lady St. Aubyn and, what was at the moment more valuable, a valiant and vastly effective ally.

18

Strangely, when Althea was in her landau on the way home to Grosvenor Square, the words that drummed in her mind were not the ones one might expect. Instead of turning over and over the facts that had overwhelmed her like a great wave on the shore, she remembered especially Lady St. Aubyn's parting advice.

They had been talking at length about the situation. The young lady that Bennie and Althea had dressed, sponsored, tried to love, certainly treated with exemplary kindness, was revealed to be—at least in all probability—a Miss Elizabeth Osborne, a cousin of the real Lucy and her companion during the eighteen months since her father had died.

"It was certainly a temptation, I see that," Lady St. Aubyn had agreed, "to have the steamship tickets and Lucy's funds, such as they were, in her hands and nowhere of her own to go to. I do not know precisely what I would have done in that event."

"Nor do I," said Althea. "But one thing is certain. She must not be allowed to continue as Lucy Rackham. Mr. Cosgrove is betrothed to her, at least for the moment, and certain others too favor her. As Lucy, that is."

"Oh, I quite agree."

"Could you please keep this private? I know I have

no need to ask, but I am so muddled I scarcely know how to go on."

"I am no gossip," said Lady St. Aubyn. "But, as I told you, my friends keep me informed. You must not allow your family's failings—and I do not now refer to Elizabeth—to rob you of what you could have that is good. Do you take my meaning?"

"Not now, ma'am. But I shall think about it."

"A family is what we are born with, unfortunately. A good marriage is what we earn ourselves."

These last were the words that sang in her thoughts.

When she neared Grosvenor Square, her spirits fell. There was an unpleasant task of monumental proportions ahead of her and she did not yet know how to deal with it. She had wasted the drive home by fanciful castles in the air, and now she was faced with ugly reality.

She stood in her own foyer and was no closer to a plan than an hour ago. Lady St. Aubyn had agreed entirely with the fact that Lucy/Elizabeth could not be permitted to continue in that identity. Deceit was no part of the Rackham philosophy. Scandal, which had flirted with Althea and her charge from time to time in the month or more since the ill-starred reception, now hovered overhead ready to break in torrents upon them.

The misdeeds laid to Lucy's door—Althea found it difficult to think of the girl as Elizabeth—were to this point peccadilloes. An escape alone to a dark garden—ill-advised, of course, but only a venial sin. The note to Noel and the invitation forbidden by Althea—a mere bagatelle. Even Noel's assault on Lucy—and Althea was more than half-convinced that Noel had violence on his drunken mind—could be dismissed as a mere undignified accident.

Comparisons, of course. The great, disastrous impersonation, the deceit, the actual fraud of Elizabeth's stealing poor dead Lucy's identity—nothing could mitigate this.

Essentially fair-minded, Althea still nursed a lingering doubt. All indications pointed to Elizabeth Osborne, the former companion, as being the person Althea knew as Lucy. Of course, the real Lucy was dead—that was a fact. Althea needed to hear confession from the girl's lips.

She was relieved to learn that Bennie had not come downstairs yet this morning. Morning? It was already noon. Althea wished to confront Elizabeth/Lucy alone. Bennie was too fond of the girl, too sentimental over Edward's orphan. Althea dreaded to think of the blow that awaited Bennie.

"Pray ask Miss Lucy"—the name stuck in her throat —"to join me in my sitting room," she instructed Tyson as she went toward the stairs.

"Miss Lucy," said Tyson disapprovingly, "has gone out."

"Oh?"

"Lord Fabyan called and invited her to take a turn in his curricle." She hesitated to ask the obvious question, but Tyson answered. "Molly is in the kitchen, eating lunch."

So the idiotic girl had gone out driving in a curricle for all to see, her maid left at home. What did she want —to be attacked again? It was strange, she thought, turning again to go upstairs. Until today she would have flown up in the boughs at such an irresponsible act. Now, Lucy, or whoever, had no real tie to her. When the impersonation was discovered, as it must be at once, her acquaintance would understand that it was not Althea's own niece who had acted in such ramshackle ways.

Our families are not our fault—Lady St. Aubyn had told her rightly.

Althea strove, understandably, to lay the blame at someone else's door: Mr. Dedman's, for not detecting the impersonation, although he had no way of doing so; Tom's, for accepting the attorney's assurances; and Caroline's, for not taking the girl under her protection at once.

And even Bennie was partly at fault, for wanting so desperately to grasp even a little of Edward, even at this late date, even after he had betrayed her love and married someone else.

By the time Althea reached her own cream-and-rose sitting room, she knew she had nobody to blame but herself. She could have said no to Tom or to Bennie, but she had not chosen to do so. And while no one could fault Althea for taking the word of her brother and Mr. Dedman as to the girl herself, yet somewhere Althea was at fault for the girl's behavior, which so often verged on the outrageous.

A short rest before lunch, a chance to gather her wits and form a specific plan, and she would before the day was over discharge her clear responsibility. First she must write at once to Tom and send the letter off today.

It was difficult to phrase her message without saying too much, and yet present a clear picture to him, one that required immediate action on his part. At length it was done, and she was just folding it when Bennie tapped at the door.

After greeting Althea, whom she had not seen that morning, Bennie informed her, "Sir Horace called this morning."

"Oh?" It was not like Sir Horace Wychley to rush to be early on the ground when something untoward had happened.

"He had much to say," Bennie confided, blushing.

"I know what he had to say, Bennie."

Bennie was taken aback. "You do? Well, I suppose you do. I should expect the most considerate actions from a gentleman like Sir Horace."

So he had not given her all the details, thought Althea, approving. "Don't be resentful, Bennie. But I am sure you are not. You of all people have such a nice sense of what is fit. I am sure you took his remarks in good part.''

Bennie stared at her. She had been downcast when she learned Sir Horace had already spoken to Althea. But there were some aspects that Bennie wished to keep private. Indeed, far from taking Althea's recommendations in good part, she was very near to becoming irritated. "Althea dear,'' she said with an appearance of calm, "I do not wish to quarrel with you. But I assure you I managed to answer Sir Horace in the proper way. I took great care not to tell him my precise reason, for I am persuaded no gentleman wishes to hear he is not paramount in a lady's regard.''

Althea was mystified. Then, slowly, she realized that Bennie was not talking about the dreadful incident at Simon's the evening before. "This is not the first time today,'' she apologized ruefully, "that I have spoken to someone at cross purposes. Dear Bennie, I have no intention now or at any time to suggest a course of action to you. I have every trust in your kindness and your sense of what is fit. Please forgive me. I should much appreciate it if you were to tell me precisely what we are talking about.''

Bennie, relieved, smiled. "I am not surprised you could not guess—you could never believe—I did not expect—''

"Bennie, I believe you are blushing!''

"The nub of it is,'' said Bennie in a burst of speech, "that Sir Horace has asked me to marry him.''

"Bennie! How marvelous! I am not at all surprised!'' Althea hugged her friend tightly and kissed her on the cheek. "You remember I told you some time ago that I thought he was interested. Tell me, when is the wedding to be? We'll begin at once to plan. I long to see you wed at St. Margaret's—''

The expression on Bennie's face stopped her, quite as much as the realization that the scandal was about to break.

When the fashionable world found out about the deception that had been practiced on them, no matter how unwittingly on the part of Althea, they would not dare to show their faces at St. Margaret's.

"But, my dear," said Bennie, "there will be no wedding."

"Bennie!" How could she have found out? But she continued, explaining, "I refused him."

Althea stared at her, stunned. "Why ever?" she demanded when she could speak again.

"I did tell you. You recall my feeling for Edward. I had had a regard for him all these years, but his death put an end to any hopes I might have had. Oh, yes, Althea. I hoped always that he would send for me."

"Dear Bennie!"

"I did not know, of course, that he had married. I confess freely that if Sir Horace had offered for me in Bath, I should quite likely have accepted. But now that Lucy has come, it is a part of Edward that has returned to me."

"I do not think so."

"Oh, but it is, you know. Although I do not trace any resemblance, yet, knowing she is his daughter—and I blush to say that in happier circumstances I think she might have been mine—well, you see that I must refuse Sir Horace."

Althea looked at her dear friend with compassion. "Oh, Bennie," she said at last, "I have such sad news for you."

"Sad news! Nothing has happened to Lucy? Althea, is she all right?"

"There has been no accident," she said literally. "But I had not thought you were excessively fond of her."

"If she is not injured, then I cannot think what your sad news could be." She looked hard at Althea. "You really wish to know my affection for her? I must be candid then." She thought for what seemed to Althea a long, long time before she resumed. "I am not precisely sure, Althea. She is Edward's daughter, of course, and I believe my feeling for her must arise from the way I feel—felt—for him."

"That is all right, then."

"Lucy is not a confiding girl. I do not know from one hour to the next what she is thinking."

Dryly, Althea said, "That may have been just as well." She pulled Bennie to her on the love seat. Holding both her hands, she said, "I do not know whether I can explain this properly, Bennie, but you must be informed."

"You frighten me."

"To begin with—"

Bennie interrupted uncharacteristically. She had sustained an emotional crisis already that day, receiving Sir Horace's offer and wanting badly to accept it. Only a strong sense of what was due to Sir Horace stood between her and contentment, if not a strongly passionate union.

"Althea, dear, pray do not dress up your news for me. Tell me quite outright what is amiss. After this morning's interview with Horace, I believe I can sustain any shock."

"Very well, Bennie. Here it is—Lucy is not Lucy."

Bennie's hands, imprisoned in hers, fluttered like caged birds. "I—I do not understand."

"How could you?" Althea agreed. "I am only now beginning to comprehend it all myself. Pray let me tell it you if I can. I am a bit muddled about some parts of the story. But I must tell you first that I called upon Lady St. Aubyn—"

"Lady St. Aubyn! She is returned from India only recently!"

"That fact is certainly germane. At any rate, this morning I went to see her, and she told me—"

The gist of the business was soon told, but not promptly believed. Bennie pulled her hands away and leapt to her feet. She began to pace in a manner reminiscent of Simon, or of Tom, her agitation extreme. "How could it be so?" she demanded, more of the air than of Althea. "Lucy dead. Edward's daughter, *dead*? Then who is this Lucy?"

She turned abruptly to Althea, her face a white mask. Only the constantly moving eyes, of an intense blue like the North Sea, reflected the turmoil within. "I don't understand, Althea. Who is this Lucy? I suppose Lucy is not even her name?"

"Her name, so I understand, is Elizabeth," Althea informed her. She had sustained the worst of the shock, at Lady St. Aubyn's, and a very good thing it was. For Bennie was going to need all of Althea's calmness to see her through. "Elizabeth Osborne."

Faced with the likelihood tht Althea was not indulging in fancy, nor on her way to Bedlam, Bennie called upon her common sense to guide her. "Very well," she said in an abruptly altered tone, "I must accept this. Lucy Rackham is dead and Elizabeth Osborne has come in her stead. Why would she wish to deceive us so?"

"For the best reason in the world, I suppose. She had no place else to go. I should judge that Elizabeth Osborne had no friends. Although a cousin, she was a servant, you know—and no matter how one dresses it up, or how well-bred she was, one must believe that she was nothing more than a maid. I think we cannot blame her too much."

"Blame her? How could anyone be so full of cruelty as to deceive us so?"

"I think we must admit that Tom and Mr. Dedman were at fault, although I do not know quite how they could have penetrated her identity. They had never known the genuine Lucy, remember."

And most of the blame lay on Edward's head, for he could long ago have made stronger efforts to recommend his daughter to his family. Some kind of description leapt to the mind.

"Oh, wicked, *wicked* girl!"

Althea had expected that Bennie would be distraught, even stunned, and she had braced herself for a stormy scene. But the depth of her revulsion was surprising, at least until Althea remembered that Bennie's disillusion was more on account of losing a slight souvenir, the tenuous connection, that was all she had left of her great love.

"To think," cried Bennie, "that I believed such a dreadful girl could be any kin to Edward. Can you credit it?"

"Yes, Bennie, dear, I can. She is, of course, no relation to the Rackhams. But she could never have succeeded in this deception, you know, had Edward been open with us."

"His family had turned him out. He had no opportunity."

"Oh, yes, he did. Tom wrote him, in care of his regiment, when our father died. Edward could have told us much about Lucy, the real Lucy, and we would never had been gulled in such a way."

Althea's brisk, matter-of-fact manner, alternating with sympathy, was effecting Bennie in the way Althea hoped. She was becoming calmer and, looking back over the last weeks, searching for clues ignored or overlooked.

"She did not always answer to her name. To Lucy, that is. Her name is—did you say, Elizabeth?"

"We think it is Elizabeth Osborne."

"But I thought you knew."

"We cannot be sure, do you think, until she admits her identity? I agree, another young lady in the tangle would be too much of a coincidence. Incidentally, Elizabeth Osborne is twenty years old."

Bennie was glum. "I am not surprised. She was too forward for a miss of eighteen, just out of the schoolroom." In a burst of confidence, Bennie delivered what seemed to Althea, later, to be the greatest surprise of the day. "Do you know, I believe I am greatly relieved. You know I tried, and I think I was kind—"

"Bennie, you are always the very essence of kindness!"

"But I could not find any affection in me for the girl. She was, at bottom, *unlikable!*"

Slowly, Althea said, "You know, Mr. Cosgrove perceived that she was afraid. He asked me what she could fear. Perhaps, when this is all out in the open and she has no reason to be afraid, she may improve in our opinions."

Bennie's expression indicated what she thought of that footless opinion. "Out in the open? The girl has brought nothing but scandal with her. What will you do next?"

"I had just finished writing to Tom when you came. I am sure he will come at once." She laughed, with rueful amusement. "It was at his behest that we received the girl. Now it is up to him to deliver us from her!"

The twinkle in Bennie's eye reflected her agreement with Althea. "Where is the girl now?"

"Out riding, I am told, for some hours now with Lord Fabyan, and only a groom."

Bennie grimaced with distaste. "No more than we can expect, I suppose. Althea, she cannot still be hopeful of marrying him?"

"Remember, she is not aware that we know her secret."

"Besides," Althea continued in a moment, "after that ugly incident last night, I wonder she trusts herself with him."

"Ugly incident?"

Althea realized that Bennie still had not been informed of the events of the after-theater party at Lord Soames' house. She hastened to relate the story.

"And whether he was carried out of his head by drink, or whether it was in fact an accident, I cannot tell you, even though I have gone over every moment in my mind. But now, of course it does not matter."

"At least, this deception will come out in time to prevent any lasting harm, either to us or to Lord Fabyan."

Althea agreed. Later, and in truth not much later, she would remember this moment. But at present, she and Bennie went down to lunch and talked of other things.

19

It was midafternoon before Lucy returned to the house. Lord Fabyan declined her invitation to come in with her, giving as his excuse that he did not want his horses to stand after some hours of activity.

In truth, he had received in the course of the afternoon's conversation with Miss Lucy Rackham an intimation of his future prospects that had left him stunned.

Lucy, on the other hand, entered the house in high spirits and lost no time in seeking out her aunt and Miss Benbow in order to acquaint them with her afternoon's achievement. Mingled with satisfaction at her triumph was a sense of relief from the constant oversight of two crabbed spinsters. In less than half a year, her fortunes had veered from nadir to pinnacle, and the ultimate goal was in her hand.

She found Aunt Althea and Miss Benbow cozily together in Althea's sitting room. If Lucy had been in the least sensitive, she must have paused on the threshold and, figuratively, sniffed the air, scenting danger.

However, since she had that afternoon achieved her greatest dream, she saw no reason to delay her triumphant announcement. She had at the beginning wished to marry well. As Lucy Rackham, with a family behind her added to her own stunning beauty, she had set her sights reasonably high. There was no reason to be greedy, and to her credit she wished for security more than great wealth.

Lord Soames had been merely a diversion. She had enjoyed this mischief of stirring up dear Aunt Althea, but Lucy was realist enough to understand that Lord Soames was beyond her reach. Besides, Lord Fabyan, unlike Lord Soames, was made of malleable material and she anticipated no difficulties in molding him to suit her. This day's work was a prime example of her expert manipulation.

She stood in the doorway of Althea's sitting room.

"Come in," said Althea pleasantly. But she could not quite bring herself to speak the girl's name—whichever name might be appropriate. "I wish to speak to you."

Lucy closed the door behind her and leaned against it, contriving to appear defenseless. "I daresay that Tyson tattled to you. There was nothing wrong. Lord Fabyan simply wished to show me his new curricle. We only drove in the park."

"Perhaps so. But you were gone for an unconscionable time. You could have driven to Windsor and back, I daresay, in the time."

"We never left the park, Aunt Althea." Lucy added demurely, "We had much to talk about."

"But little to the point, I suspect. Unless, as I must suppose, he wished to apologize for his sottish behavior of last night?"

Bennie eyed Althea warily. She had expected confrontation probably of a fiery nature and had braced her gentle spirit to face the storm. Bennie at bottom was the sweetest of persons, having a kindly nature and a tolerant outlook. But Lucy/Elizabeth's deception had insulted her sense of justice, and at this moment justice took precedence over kindliness. But Althea seemed reluctant to join battle.

Lucy, on the other hand, seemed inordinately pleased with herself. "Yes, that incident was discussed." She shot a sharp glance at Bennie. "I suppose Aunt Althea told you that Lord Fabyan was just a wee bit foxed?"

Bennie nodded, unable to trust her voice.

"He fell against me. Foolishly I thought I could hold him up, but he was much too heavy."

Althea inquired, "Then it really was an accident?"

"Oh, yes, an accident. I certainly would not wish to accuse Noel of—anything sinister, would I? Especially since he has offered for me."

Althea's disbelief, thought Lucy, was hardly flattering. Did she think I could not carry it off? "Offered!" cried Althea. "Marriage?"

Lucy said innocently, "Oh, did I use the wrong word? Offered for, means marriage, does it not? At any rate, I shall marry him."

"And Mr. Cosgrove, whom your father wished you to marry?"

Only Bennie heard the slight stress on "your father."

"Mr. Cosgrove means nothing to me. No one knew I would meet Lord Fabyan, how could they? Mr. Cosgrove may return to Ireland as far as I am concerned. From what he has told me, I should not like it above half."

Althea and Bennie exchanged glances. Knowing what they now knew, they were astonished that they had not seen her for what she was before this. And yet, as each of them remembered oddments flung to the surface of memory like flotsam, the signs were there, if one had been suspicious enough. Now, it seemed to them both that the very air surrounding the girl shouted to the high heavens—deceit!

Lucy smiled brilliantly at them. "I must hurry and dress. Will you be in for dinner? I have invited Lord Fabyan."

She had turned to leave, her hand on the door latch.

Althea's voice reached her. "Elizabeth!"

"Yes?" Lucy responded instantly. Then, she stiffened, arrested, for the moment it took for her to realize what she had done. *Elizabeth!* To come so far and fall into such a simple trap!

"Best come back and sit down," advised Althea. "We have much to talk about, Elizabeth Osborne."

The girl turned, her face drawn and white, her violet eyes miserable. "How did you find out?" she whispered.

As an admission of her identity, it could not have been clearer.

Bennie snorted, "It's all true, then. You are wicked and cruel. I did not really believe it until now." She glanced apologetically at Althea. "You cannot deny the proof."

Althea pointed to the chair opposite her, and the girl came, one step at a time as though each foot must be activated by an exercise of will. Seated, she was not defeated.

"Proof? You have no proof of anything, Miss Benbow. Besides, proof of what? I am Lucy Rackham, you have all the papers I brought. There is proof for you."

Althea shook her head pityingly. "Do you truly put your trust in legalities, in documents? I must tell you there are persons in London, of impeccable reputation, who are acquainted with you, and with my niece Lucy. It would require only a few minutes to bring them here. I am sure their identification of you—as Elizabeth Osborne, of course—would be considered valid."

Elizabeth caught her breath in a sob. In a small voice, she protested, "Noel will not believe you."

That whimpering remark, Althea considered, did not deserve a reply. Instead, she said, "I have already informed my brother of your imposture. What happens to you on that head must be his decision. There will of course be no question of an alliance with Lord Fabyan."

Elizabeth put her hands to her face and broke into noisy weeping. Even Bennie was moved by the girl's obvious wretchedness.

"What harm did I do Lucy?" came to them in muffled tones.

"Great harm," said Bennie with great and remote dignity, "has been done to us all."

At last the painful scene was over. Elizabeth—it was even yet easier to think of her as Lucy—had departed with slow step, like a rheumatic old woman. There was meat for philosophy, thought Althea, in the sudden reversal of fortune that had taken place in the girl's life in the course of the last hour.

From Lucy Rackham, pampered daughter of a substantial family, affianced to Lord Fabyan, to Elizabeth Osborne, impostor, in disgrace. The alteration in her cirumstances was a tragedy for the girl. Althea prayed it would be less damaging to the others around her.

Bennie followed Elizabeth out, to see her safely to her room, leaving Althea with a monstrous pounding headache.

She had sent for Tom. Now she was consumed by an overpowering wish for Simon, not merely to throw herself on his chest and feel his powerful embrace, offering protection and comfort. Also in her mind was the conviction that she would get on much better with Simon at her side, his strong intellect helping her to see clearly her course in this matter, and—very simply —simply to be here.

She would send a note to him asking him to wait on her. She must tell him, of course, about the fraud Elizabeth had perpetrated on them all. He would in all likelihood take steps to undeceive his nephew.

She sat up with a start. There were things to do. She must send to Lord Fabyan, putting him off for dinner. Lord Fabyan had unaccountably offered for Lucy. But now that Althea had leisure to consider the news Elizabeth had brought an hour since, she could begin to wonder at the circumstances that had brought the arrangement about.

She strongly suspected that the girl had manipulated Noel into the offer, but how could she have done so? Then Althea recalled the strange look on her face the night before, when they had set her on her feet, tugging the torn edges of the saffron gown into decent covering. Elizabeth's eyes had held an enigmatic expression, a calculating look that Althea had not liked at the time. Now, that recollection, combined with the patently insincere voice this afternoon saying, "I certainly would not wish to accuse Noel of anything sinister," revealed a great deal.

He must have thought he had no choice—marry Lucy or face the scandalous report of an attempted rape upon a young lady of quality. Expressed in that way, the boy had no choice. At least now, she thought, he would soon be freed of that incubus.

Althea closed her eyes, hoping to ease her headache. Would they ever be able to sort out all of Elizabeth Osborne's falsehoods?

In the long run, it probably would not matter in the least.

20

In the short run, the untangling of Elizabeth's false-hoods mattered a great deal.

The next morning, Althea visited the girl in her room. The maid Molly opened the door at her rap, looking frightened. "It is only I, Molly," said Althea pleasantly. "I see you have brought Miss Lucy her breakfast." She nodded in dismissal, and Molly fled incontinently.

"Good morning, Elizabeth," said Althea.

"Make up your mind, ma'am," said Elizabeth insolently. "Am I Miss Lucy or am I Miss Elizabeth?"

"You know that your standing in this house is equivocal. You must not assume, simply because I do not wish to make the servants privy to what is still a family secret, that you are to continue as before."

"Why not? Nobody knows that you've been prying about."

"Whatever sympathy I might have felt for you, Elizabeth, recalling that you were quite at the end of your rope when Lucy died—yes, I know that Lucy died of the plague in Bombay—has quite vanished in the face of your impertinence. You would do better to enlist my support when my brother arrives."

Elizabeth was not in her best looks this morning. Her eyes were red and swollen, her cheeks puffy. Even her hair had lost its shine. Althea could have been brought to a high pitch of compassion for the girl, adrift as it were in a strange city, trying to survive.

Survive—Althea was struck by an unwelcome idea.
"The plague, Elizabeth. I wonder that you did not take
it yourself, nursing Lucy as she died."

"I—I must have had it as an infant," suggested
Elizabeth lamely.

"I see. I would prefer to believe you, of course,
although I must admit I have no grounds on which to
do so."

"Can't you just leave me alone?"

She watched Elizabeth for a moment. Clearly the girl
appeared contrite and broken. But once the fabric of
trust is torn in one place, there is little substance to
any of the rest of it. Althea did not know what to
believe.

"At any rate, Elizabeth," said Althea, "you are to be
confined to your room until Lord Darley arrives. What
happens after that will be his decision."

"When will that be?"

"Tomorrow, in all likelihood. You have not long to
wait."

A fleeting smile crossed the girl's face—of relief, no
doubt, that her imprisonment would not be long.

Later that morning, an expected visitor was
announced. Althea went to receive Lord Soames in the
drawing room. She had an unpleasant half-hour ahead
of her, but her pleasure in seeing Simon mitigated the
prospect.

"Good morning," she greeted him. "How good of
you to respond so promptly to my note."

"Note? More like a summons."

Taken aback, she stammered, "S-summons? I know
I was at wit's end in framing it, but—"

"I suppose," said Simon harshly, and now she could
see that his features were set along grim lines, "that
you asked me here to listen to all the things that were
impossible for you to say the other night. Well, I must
endure, I suppose."

Her temper flared. "I wonder that you came, then, if
you expect me to scold you."

A glint, of a kind well-known to her, appeared in his
amber eyes. "We should not deal at all if you refrained
from scolding. It occurs to me that you have lost the
art of civil conversation."

"I should have known," she said bitterly, "that all
you can think to do is ring a peal over me. Very well,
have your say and be done with it."

A quiver in her tone struck him like a knife turning
in his chest. He looked more closely at her and seized
her hands. "My dear, what is amiss? Believe me, I had
no intention of hurting you any more than I have
already done."

The tender concern in his voice completed her
undoing.

"Good God, Althea, don't cry! You know I cannot
abide to see you weep! What is amiss? I wager it is
that abominable girl! What's she done?" Feeling that a
light touch might be welcome, he added, "Has she
eloped with Sir Horace? I wager Bennie will have
something to say to that."

"She said, No, and it's all for nothing!"

Rightly discerning that a disaster of major proportions was about to be narrated, since the less sense his
darling Althea made, the more ominous the prospect,
he pulled her to sit on the sofa and sat beside her.
Turning her face into his shoulder, he allowed her to
sob without hindrance. When a hiccuping sound
reached his ear, familiar long since with her habits, he
knew that she was recovering.

At length she pulled away from him and sat straight.
He regarded her carefully and, seeing that she was
once more restored, allowed himself a slight, amused
smile. "Now, then, my dear watering pot, shall I have
an explanation of this sudden storm?"

"Oh, Simon," she said with a watery smile, "why can
you not always be this—this comfortable?"

"I shall endeavor to improve," he said gravely. "Provided, of course—"

She gave the proviso the measure of attention it deserved, and ignored it. "There is such dreadful news! No, no, no one is ill or dead. Except, of course, my niece Lucy."

"Good God!" he exclaimed. "From that fall the other night?"

"Oh, no. That wasn't Lucy."

Baffled, and holding his ordinarily short temper under tight rein, he leaned back, folded his arms, and said, "I shall listen with fascination to whatever you have to tell me. But my girl, I warn you, an expeditious narrative will please me best."

"I shall try, Simon. I admit the entire matter strains credulity, but—" Catching a gleam in his eye that she knew well, she set about forthwith on explaining, as well as she could, the entire matter of Lucy/Elizabeth.

She was gratified by his intense attention to her story. Only when she finished, telling him even of her visit to Elizabeth that morning—"I do find it hard not to call her Lucy, you know, even now"—and her intention to keep the girl confined until Tom arrived.

Chafing under the necessity of keeping silent until he had heard the entire tale, Simon burst out, "Tom! What can he do? He is the cause of this entire maladroit business!"

"Surely not? He could not know that Lucy had died!"

"I make no point about that. But he and his precious wife—" Simon remembered that this line of discussion, two years ago, had led to the worst time in his life, when Althea had told him bluntly that she could imagine no fate worse than being yoked to a man with such a vicious temper.

"Well," he said, avoiding her eyes, "I am sure that blame cannot be attached to anyone, except the wretched girl. The place for the minx is Newgate. Or possibly Bedlam, if we are to judge by her conviction that she could succeed in such a fraud."

"But she nearly has," Althea pointed out. "Indeed, she informed us yesterday that Noel had offered."

Storm clouds gathered in Simon's brow. "Offered? I shall have something to say on that head."

"I think we do not need to pursue that, Simon. As soon as Noel learns her identity, he will cry off."

"Do you know, Althea, I am quite weary of my family? I am persuaded that your family also is not giving you much pleasure at the moment?"

"Not much." In a burst of frankness, she said, "Do you know, Simon, at one point I could have strangled Tom."

"I wish I had known. You might not have been able to encompass it alone."

With satisfaction, he heard her gurgling chuckle and knew that she was herself again. Whatever the miserable wench upstairs had done to Althea's sensibilities was likely past repair. But at least he could see that her future prospects were serene, secure, and to the best of his ability, happy.

"I seem to remember," he said, "some very odd remark you made about Sir Horace."

"Sir Horace? Did I?"

"I think the words, 'she said, No, and it was all for naught,' were prominent. My curiosity is piqued. Who said, No?"

So she must tell him about Sir Horace's proposal to Bennie and dear Bennie's gallant loyalty to her first love. "And of course, her sacrifice is all for nothing, for the girl isn't Edward's!"

"A convoluted piece of logic," he judged, "but I can accept it. However, I do not think we need concern ourselves with Miss Benbow's reasoning, do you? I feel quite certain that Sir Horace will renew his attentions when he is informed of this unfortunate deception." He looked closely at her. "You surely did not think you could prevent Miss—whatever her name is—"

"Elizabeth Osborne."

"Miss Osborne's daring venture from becoming common knowledge, did you? There is no possible way to explain Miss Lucy Rackham's withdrawal from society in any way that will pass muster."

"No, Simon, I do not truly think so. But perhaps Caroline will suggest some subterfuge."

"Caroline be—" He stopped abruptly, then continued in a mild manner, "I am sure I hope she will."

He leaned toward Althea and took both her hands in his. He looked deep into her gray eyes, and the pregnant silence between them lengthened. Her breath came shallowly and she could hardly hear for the drumming of her blood in her head. Her lips parted slightly.

"Althea—" he said in a voice roughened by emotion.

The door to the drawing room burst open. "Miss Rackham!" Emma Fabyan cried shrilly. "What are you going to do about it?"

I'll say yes yes yes, Althea screamed, but only in her mind. Simon had leapt to his feet in stunned surprise at the vehement interruption, and thunderclouds came down on his features. If Simon were ever to dispatch someone in the heat of the moment, Althea thought, he would look just like this.

Gathering her wits together, Althea stared at her visitor. Lady Fabyan was indeed distraught, to judge from her appearance. Her green bonnet was not set straight and surely she could not have planned to wear it with that shocking shade of blue muslin!

"What on earth, Emma, can you be thinking of?" roared Simon.

"I want Miss Rackham to answer me."

Conciliation was called for here, not only for Simon's sake, thought Althea, but also because the woman was truly distressed. "I shall be pleased to answer you," she said in an effort to be calm, "if I knew what the question was."

"The question is, What have you done with my son? You sent him off with that dreadful, forward girl. I have never thought highly of your family, Miss Rackham, but I did suppose that you had more control over your niece than it appears."

Bewildered, Althea said, "But I do not know what you talk of." She suspected darkly that Noel had made a mishmash of telling his mother he had made that ill-starred offer of marriage to Lucy. No, to Elizabeth. But that wasn't right, for Noel still thought she was Lucy!

"I'm talking about eloping."

"Eloping?" Althea echoed.

"You've lost your senses!" shouted Simon.

"I'm talking about Gretna Green, Miss Rackham. You, Simon, I shall ignore, for if it were not for you, Noel would not have been exposed to the wiles of that —that person!" Having delivered herself of the worst insult she could think of, she burst into tears.

Since Emma Fabyan had left the drawing room door open behind her, and Tyson, excessively curious, had been slow to close it, the uproar could be heard over a large part of the house. Drawn by the logical expectation that yet another disaster had struck, Bennie hurried down the stairs to the center of the hubbub. Peering through the drawing room door, she was astonished to see Lady Fabyan, handkerchief to her eyes, seated in a large chair pounding her free hand rhythmically on the arm.

Lord Soames frowned at Althea, but Bennie believed he did not see her, being intent on his own thoughts. Althea, stony-faced, was approaching the door.

"Dear Bennie, you are just in time. Lady Fabyan has come with the most infamous tale. She insists that Lord Fabyan had run away with El—with Lucy. I cannot believe it myself, but I suppose we must make sure."

"I shall go, Althea," offered Bennie. "You must stay with your guests."

Althea looked behind her at Simon and his sister. "Guests! More like judge and jury, I warrant you. Lady Fabyan feels that I must have promoted such a ramshackle escapade. You know—and I am sure Simon knows, for I confided in him—that even the most staid marriage arrangement cannot be countenanced, to say nothing of a flight to the border."

Bennie looked apprehensively around for Tyson. Althea seemed recklessly indiscreet in her talk before the servants, but she supposed that they would learn soon enough that miss was a fraud and an impostor! There seemed no danger, however, that Tyson had overheard, since Lord Soames had engaged him in conversation.

"I'll just be a moment," promised Bennie, and hurried toward the stairs.

"Now, Emma," said Althea bracingly, "do try to compose yourself. Your son has not eloped with my niece, you may be sure of that." Very sure indeed, Althea told herself, but if one meant Elizabeth, one could not be positive.

"She has been a menace from the start," wailed Emma, failing entirely to pull herself together as recommended to her by Althea. "Little did you know what a monster you unleashed upon your friends."

Althea considered a number of telling retorts, discarding them all. Her hesitation gave Simon the opportunity he wanted. "Typical of you, Emma. You find no fault in that green hobbledehoy of yours. If he had taken after the Hallecks, instead of his loose screw of a father, you'd not now be mewling over him."

The ungentle treatment worked its intended miracle. "You dare to say so! I do not say Noel is without flaw—"

"You had better not!"

"But surely even you could see how the chit ran after him. He could hardly call his soul his own."

"Precisely my point, Emma," said her brother frankly. "If he'd had any kind of sense, or even a rudimentary adherence to some basic principles, he would have sent her packing. He was already betrothed, dammit, to a girl worth five of him.''

The quarrel might have gone on at length, but since it was deteriorating rapidly, in all likelihood it would have degenerated to the level of nursery squabbles. It was prevented from such a fate by the arrival of Bennie returning from upstairs.

One glance at her frantic eyes in her white face was enough to inform them that the girl was indeed not in the house.

"She was confined to her room," fumed Althea.

"Obviously she did not stay there," said Simon. "Can her maid tell you if any of her garments are missing?"

Under Simon's questioning, certain facts were revealed. Elizabeth had been gone from the house for more than two hours, having, with Molly's connivance, packed a small hand satchel with a dress, a warm shawl, and an extra pair of shoes, and dressed in Molly's own plain gray dress and black shawl, had stolen through the kitchen, when Cook was leaning with concentration over the spit, and left the house by the mews lane.

"And by now they'll be halfway to the border," wailed Emma.

"Your notion of geography is rudimentary," snorted Simon. "Emma, do go home and leave the cub to me."

"Simon, do you think you may catch them?" asked Althea.

"Even if they had gone to the border, I will hope to forestall the marriage. I have sent your footman for my curricle and my blacks. The vehicle should be here shortly and I shall be off."

"Simon," she said in a lower voice, glancing warily at Emma, "I truly did have the girl confined to her room. But her maid is such a partisan of hers."

"Do not listen to Emma. Of course you did not abet this mad scheme. We both know that. Never fear, I shall bring them back."

Emma overheard the last few words. "Bring them back? Married, I shouldn't wonder. And then what will you do, Miss Rackham? You will be well advised to make little of it, for I shall have much to say against any great celebration, mark my words!"

Althea decided there was no reasoning with Lady Fabyan. In truth, as she recalled the years of their acquaintance, there never had been any use in measured argument. Instead, she said to Simon, "I shall just get my cloak and bonnet, and I shall be ready by the time your curricle arrives."

Simon frowned. "Cloak and bonnet? Surely you do not expect to go with me?"

"Indeed I do. If you were to reflect upon it, you would see that my presence is necessary."

"I don't admit that at all!"

"Then," she said calmly, "you do not expect to overtake them?"

"That does not follow! I told you I would overtake them. But I shall be traveling fast!"

"I should hope so. But I wonder, Simon, how you will deal when you catch them up? You surely see the necessity of having a respectable female along to preserve appearances?"

"She is right, Simon!" Emma burst out. "I shall go!"

"Good God, I am beset by headstrong females!"

"And quite right," said Althea with her sweetest smile. "Bennie, would you please send for my dark-gray cloak and bonnet? I think an unobtrusive costume will be best."

She was dressed and at the door by the time Simon's curricle and his glossy matched blacks arrived. Emma was still trying to persuade Simon to take her with him. "He is my son! You do not understand him!"

"Nor," said Simon harshly, "do you, or you would keep him on a tighter rein!"

In the end, as she had foreseen, Simon was forced to take her with him. Her argument about the need for proper chaperonage of Elizabeth—she had better, until the matter was straightened out, continue to think of her as Lucy—carried weight. But, as she had also foreseen, the deciding factor was Simon's realization that if the seat were not occupied already by Althea, then Lady Fabyan would carry the day.

"Will you be warm enough, Althea?" he asked mildly. He knew when he was beaten.

"Yes, Simon, I am sure I will."

21

Some two hours before Lady Fabyan burst into Althea's drawing room to the discomfiture of the two persons therein, in a small reception of hired lodgings in a nearby street, Claude Cosgrove lingered over his morning coffee.

He was pondering over his next move. He had come to London at the behest of Mr. Dedman, a friend of his father's. He had long known about the betrothal arrangement made by his father and Colonel Rackham, but as he had told Althea, it meant little to him. He considered himself bound by it, however, at least until some crisis arose that might cause him to assess the arrangement anew.

Such a crisis had now arisen.

When he had first met Miss Lucy, he had, as had every man in London, been bowled over by those glorious violet eyes and the perfection of her features. He considered himself as a fortunate man.

Every eligible male in London beat a path to the door of the Rackham house in Grosvenor Square. The competition did not particularly daunt Claude, because he believed that persistence would in the end pay off. As time went on and he was in company with her frequently, his feelings toward her underwent a change.

Miss Lucy was a passable female possessed of an unearthly beauty which would last at the most five years. He was not impressed by her charm or her learning, neither lack making any difference to a man whose own accomplishments were meager.

He was aware, though, of a great appeal in her. Never greatly articulate, he could not put his yearnings into words, but he sensed a quality in her that he could identify only as "fear." And in his prosaic way, he stood ready to fight whatever dragons were required. In pursuance of the protective strain now dominant in him, he had been on hand to pull Noel off the supine Miss Lucy.

He did not mind that she had not thanked him. He had seen more than anyone knew, and the story of an accidental fall, which Lucy tried to break, did not convince him. If Lucy wanted it that way, however, she would not find him objecting.

He could not avoid realizing, though, that Lucy's attentions did not lie in his direction. She obviously favored Lord Fabyan or Lord Soames. Claude did not think Lord Soames a great gaby to be taken in by a young miss, but it seemed evident that whoever captured Lucy, it would not be Claude Cosgrove.

Even after the man had attacked her, Lucy still favored young Fabyan. Claude was thus meditating over coffee growing cold whether it was time to return to his green acres in County Meath and put London and Lucy right out of his mind.

He was interrupted by a note brought to him by his manservant, Boyce. "The messenger said there was no answer."

He puzzled over the scribbled words for some time. Even when he deciphered them, the message did not make much sense. "Follow me as soon as you can. Lucy and I off to Gretna. Come to Netherton Magna. Inquire White Pony. Desperate." It was signed in a scrawl that he construed as "Fabyan."

Never hasty in judgment, Claude considered the message. Fabyan was eloping with Lucy, that was obvious, and on their way to Gretna Green. Being somewhat of a stranger to England, he knew only that

the place of hasty marriages was north of the border,
and therefore in Scotland.

Very well. Fabyan asked his help, which, if it were a
matter of Fabyan alone, he must refuse. However, if
Lucy were with him, then Claude had a paramount responsibility to rescue her, again. Surely only a lackwit
would hare off across country with a man who had
within the previous forty-eight hours attempted her
virtue.

Claude prepared, in his deliberate fashion, to pursue.

His first call was in Mount Street, where Miss More
received him almost at once. She was obviously surprised to see him, for it was midmorning, an uncon-
ventional hour for a mere acquaintance to call.

"I must apologize for calling on you without first
seeking your aunt's permission, but I have a matter of
some urgency to discuss."

"What can it be?" she wondered. "Pray sit down."

"Please excuse me, Miss More, for I must not
delay." He had had sufficient time to mull over the odd
circumstances of Lord Fabyan's message. Surely a
man who was intent upon removing his intended bride
from her family, to accomplish a ramshackle marriage,
would not send word to someone he knew only slightly.
Claude was not certain whether he was setting out to
rescue Lucy from her kidnapper, or Lord Fabyan.

At any rate, he must make haste. "I am at a dis-
advantage, Miss More. I have occasion to go to a place
called Netherton Magna, and I have not the slightest
notion of how to get there."

"Netherton Magna! That is quite near my own
home." Curiosity vied with propriety and won out.
"May I ask what you will do at Netherton Magna? It is
quite the smallest of villages, with only an inn—"

"The White Pony, I gather?"

"Yes! How do you know that? It is not an inn of the
first water, and while Lockhart keeps a respectable
house, I should be much surprised to find his reputation had reached London."

Mr. Cosgrove reddened. He was not adept at evasion. His life till now had been straightforward, honest, and simple. Now that he had made Lucy's acquaintance, he found himself prey to alarums and excursions, to emotions he had never felt before, and to be honest, to a spice in his life that he would not like to lose.

He was ill-equipped to parry the probing questions put to him by Miss More. To begin with, he had not yet learned the location of Netherton Magna. "I fear my business there is not fit for delicate ears," he said earnestly. "If you could set me in the right direction, I should be most grateful."

Dorcas had, of course, had her first Season the year before, and had found no one she liked quite as well as Noel Fabyan. She suspected that his character was not strong, but she thought he was ideally suited for a country life, as she was herself. The even tenor of her ways had not previously been disturbed, but the advent of Miss Lucy Rackham had been as devastating as an earthquake to Noel, and inevitably to Dorcas.

She had come to town simply to seek diversion from her unhappiness. Instead, she had come to the conviction that Lucy was the worst possible wife for Noel and had found in herself a steely determination to rescue him. She had thought his attachment to Lucy was weakening.

Mr. Cosgrove's visit alarmed her anew. Netherton Magna was near the Fabyan estates as well as the More lands. Darley Hall was not far away and the substantially larger holdings of Lord Soames spread across the rolling countryside.

"Mr. Cosgrove, I am persuaded that your errand to Netherton Magna is of the first importance. But do you see, you are speaking of people I know, of my own neighborhood. Pray tell me what has gone wrong at home?"

He could not resist the appeal in her blue eyes. He

showed her, since there was no help for it, Noel's message.

"It's Noel's hand!" she cried at once. She deciphered the scrawl in much less time than Claude had required. "Eloping? With Lucy? What fustian!"

"I do not think so."

"Noel would never do such a ramshackle thing! Depend upon it," Dorcas exclaimed, her eyes angry, "that Lucy has suborned him in some way. We must stop them!"

"I have every intention of doing so," said Mr. Cosgrove deliberately, "if you will be good enough to give me directions."

She thought for a moment. Then, clearly coming to a decision, she replied, "Of course I will! Just let me get my cloak and leave a message for my aunt!"

"Oh, no! That is to say, Miss More, you cannot mean that you wish to go with me. I am persuaded that is not at all the thing to do."

She turned at the door. "You really cannot do without me."

"But—"

"How will you get to Netherton Magna?"

She did not wait for his answer. In truth, there was no answer possible to give. Surely there were persons in London—in all likelihood, dozens—who knew the way to Netherton Magna. However, to seek them out would be time-consuming, even supposing he had the first notion of how to go about finding them, and in the interests of haste he must surrender to Miss More's decision.

Really, he thought, he would be glad of her company, no matter how inconvenient or how improper such a journey might prove to be.

Dorcas was a marvel of swiftness, and in less than a quarter of an hour she reappeared, dressed in a dark-green bombazine carriage dress trimmed with a *rouleau* of mingled crepe and silk in the same color. Her

Parisian bonnet was already tied with ribbons under her chin. Her maid, a shawl hastily thrust around her shoulders, was following, a shocked expression on her face, holding a pelerine of enormous size.

"Please, Miss Dorcas, stop a moment—"

Impatiently Dorcas let her maid envelop her in a cloak in the newest fashion, and then declared herself ready. Three on the seat were a tight fit.

Trusting in her maid's discretion, Dorcas said nothing until Mr. Cosgrove had maneuvered the curricle out of Mount Street and on the road to Barnet.

"How clever of you to get such an early start," she told him. "Do you know how far ahead of us they are?"

He glanced at her. He had expected hysterics from her when she learned about Noel's nefarious scheme, but she bore no resemblance to a jilted bride. Instead, her spirits seemed exceptionally high.

Feeling that an explanation might be welcome, she said, "Do you see, Noel is asking you to rescue him. Does that sound like a man in thrall to his intended bride? I confess I have been much troubled since he told me he did not wish to marry me—"

"I should think so!"

"But now you see I was right all along."

Mr. Cosgrove was at sea. "Right?"

"I have wondered—indeed, I have really thought it certain these last days—that Noel was becoming just a little weary of her. I daresay she had not noticed, but I know him well and he is prone to take fancies."

Now that the road lay straighter and without much traffic, Mr. Cosgrove let his Irish bays out.

"How far is it to Netherton Magna?" This was not the first time he had inquired, but now that they were advancing on their way, he had hopes of an answer.

"We shall be there comfortably in time for a nuncheon. Mrs. Lockhart will do us well, I am persuaded, for we are quite old friends." The ensuing silence provided opportunity for too many unpleasant thoughts, in which Noel's failings figured largely.

"What magnificent horses you have," she exclaimed in admiring tones, "so perfectly matched. I am sure we will have a comfortable ride."

"I bred these horses myself," said Mr. Cosgrove with quiet pride.

Dorcas expressed intelligent interest in his agricultural projects, and an hour passed swiftly.

"Surely," said Mr. Cosgrove, at last returning to the topic uppermost in his thought, "we shall not have time to eat at the White Pony? I am persuaded we must overtake them very soon, but they have likely two hours' start on us."

"I should think," said Dorcas judiciously, "that Noel will not be traveling fast."

He was apprehensive. Miss More did not seem in the least troubled. She must not understand the gravity of the situation, for any right-minded female would shudder at the outrage perpetrated on a young lady by a gentleman who persuaded her to an elopement. A marriage over the anvil was almost the same as no marriage at all.

Yet Fabyan had sent him the note, a message that could only be construed as a plea for intervention. Miss More had made certain remarks that puzzled him. While he could hazard a guess at the thoughts that lay behind her cryptic remarks, he preferred to leave nothing to chance. He must inquire, but he was not quite sure what questions to ask.

Barnet had come and gone in a whirl of houses, inns, old church, and they were on their way to Hatfield along the Great North Road before he found the right words.

At that moment, more than an hour behind Mr. Cosgrove and Dorcas More, Simon's smart curricle stood at the door, his famous blacks harnessed abreast, and Althea was handed up onto the seat.

Simon took the reins in his strong hands, and with a swift glance at his passenger sent the blacks on their first steps toward the anvil at Gretna Green.

The blacks under perfect control, they threaded through the lively throngs in the streets, soon leaving the city behind.

They traversed Barnet without stopping. "Should we not inquire someplace?" Althea wondered. "I know it is too soon to change horses, but perhaps they stopped to bait? I am sure Lucy had nothing to eat before she left the house." Then, the words wrung from her by strong emotion, she exclaimed, "That wretched girl!"

"If you were—whatever her name is—would you wish to take time to eat when you were only this far from London?"

"No," said Althea promptly, "you are right, of course. I should be terrified lest pursuit be close behind."

They were on their way to Hatfield. "My blacks are good for two stages," Simon informed her. "If Noel is driving those cattle he picked up last week at Tattersall's, we may be fortunate enough to come upon them in any ditch."

"Surely not!"

"I assure you. Noel is as poor a judge of horseflesh as he is of women."

Stung, Althea retorted, "Women are to be judged as to their merits like any cattle? I should have expected more—more fastidiousness from you."

"You might well do so. I had the excellent taste to offer for you, did I not?"

"On my merits as a stayer?" she said tartly.

"I should have been badly mistaken had I done so. Although I believe," he added, more humbly than she had ever known him to be, "I was the one who foundered."

After a moment, Althea said in a subdued voice, "The fault was not yours."

"Then, whose? It was never yours."

Astonished, Althea stared at him. He did not turn to look at her, however, keeping his eyes on the road ahead. They were swiftly overtaking a coach making good speed.

Althea watched the distance between them diminish at an alarming rate. "How unfortunate!" she exclaimed as she recognized the maroon-and-black body signifying that the vehicle was one of His Majesty's mail coaches. "Now we shall be delayed greatly!"

She reckoned without Simon's determination to overtake his nephew. He reached for the horn and blew a single warning blast. "Simon, you're not going to pass!"

"Why not?" he said simply. "There is room."

"But it's a mail coach!" These were special vehicles that carried only mail, and occasionally a passenger. They traveled on fast schedules, allowing nothing to delay them. It was said that clocks could be set by the passing of the mail. It was folly to overtake them.

"If only no one is coming!"

She looked fearfully at the sides of the road. She had no wish to be overturned in a ditch, even though the blacks were in no danger of foundering, as Noel's were reputed to be. The hedges on either side were already covered with dust churned up by the constant traffic. By mid-June the leaves would be thickly white.

The stage loomed larger and Simon swung out to pass. She closed her eyes. Not ordinarily a religious person, she considered the present moment one for petition, if ever there was one. They were past.

"Goodness, Simon, I had quite forgot that you drive to an inch," she said when she could get her breath.

"I wish your memory were not quite so selective," he said quietly. "I could choose other subjects which are better to forget."

Once again they were coming very close to a point where, this time, there would be no turning back. If

Simon still wanted to marry her, if he were still as passionately in love with her as he had professed to be once, then she would accept him, gladly, and never look back.

But he had not said so, these weeks since he had come to London, hanging out, as he had told her, for a wife—a docile wife. He seemed to have abandoned his search, as far as she could tell, but what if he had not?

Suppose, she posed the question to herself, he was simply paying his attentions to her in order to be in a position to thwart any marriage between her niece and his nephew. This mad journey to the north on the trail of the runaways would culminate in freeing Noel to return to his obligation to Dorcas.

What, then, of Simon? Would this be the end of her own hopes? Suddenly, her self-assurance, nurtured by Simon's attentions, drained away like raindrops in a sandy field. She suspected, with a quite dreadful lowering of her spirits, that she had misread his intentions.

If the break two years before had been miserable, the immediate prospect for Althea bordered on catastrophic.

Venice would not be far enough to travel, being only a month away from Simon's presence. Perhaps she could seek out Lady Hester Stanhope and join her Oriental court!

They were at Hatfield.

Inquiries at the several inns elicited the information that a black curricle and a pair of goers—real corkers, they were!—had stopped for a nuncheon. Simon returned to the curricle, where Althea was holding the reins.

"They're only an hour ahead of us," he concluded.

"But do they not have fresh horses now?"

"No, apparently not. The stable boy is an idiot. He seemed to think Noel's cattle were good for another stage. He must have sold the ones he bought last week, on my advice."

"Of course," said Althea, her recent reflections making her a trifle testy. "Too bad he did not follow your advice in all things."

"Listen to me, my girl, I have had enough of your complaints!"

"Complaints? I had considered my remarks only a recitation of plain fact." Instantly apologetic, she added, "Simon, do let us not quarrel. I am persuaded that we will overtake them, and all will be well. Truly I do not know how I should go on without you."

The irritation in his amber eyes softened to good humor. "Very well, my dear. You have the right of it. I am to blame for Noel and you, my dear girl, you are to blame for nothing."

He swung up onto the box and took the reins from her hands. "I shall not let you blame yourself for that young criminal. There was no way you could have unmasked her. I shall not revile you for this, if you forgive me that cawker I have for a nephew. A shocking loose screw, no doubt of it. Takes after his father. Did you know him?"

They moved out of Hatfield toward Welwyn. "If Noel plans to change horses, Welwyn seems to be the place most likely. At any rate we shall inquire there."

With that, she had to be content.

In the event, they never reached Welwyn.

A mile outside Hatfield, the road sloped down toward the bridge over the River Lea, to rise on the other side and continue on toward the north.

The slope was not steep enough to require the placing of skids on the rear wheel to slow the descent, but nonetheless Simon drew his pair to a halt at the brow of the hill.

"Good God, look there!"

"An accident? How dreadful! Someone may be hurt!"

"That's not the worst of it. Our abominable runaways may have escaped us by this mischance."

"I quite see that they have in all likelihood passed through before the accident. But we must see what we may do here to assist the injured."

"No injured. At least, if there were, they have been conveyed to another location. This is an old wreck."

"Old? How can you say so? This is a well-traveled road and surely the coach would have been removed by now."

"In all probability, it happened at least an hour ago. You see the horses have been cut loose and taken away. But we shall doubtless learn what we need to know from the workman approaching us."

One of the workmen toiling with diligence to right the coach and move it off the bridge had left his labors to approach the smart curricle and splendid pair he saw halted at the top of the rise.

"Begging your favor, my lord," he said after a quick glance at the nonesuch holding the reins, "you can't get by." He cast a swift glance at the lady and added in kind explanation, "No room."

"Are we the only wayfarers inconvenienced by the idiot driver?"

"Aye, idiot you may say, sir. Not much of a slope you'd think, being an expert as even I can see, sir, with the reins. But yon coachman came down roaring like it was a straightaway flat as a field, and did hit the 'butment, took off a couple of stone, and overturned the lot." He caught Simon's stern eye and quickly provided the answer to his question. "A matter of two curricles, with some handsome cattle, at least one of 'em, and a wagon. Sent 'em that way." He gestured toward the opening of a narrow country road bordered by hedges heavy with fresh dust.

An odd expression passed over Simon's features, and he exclaimed under his breath, "Hadn't thought he had that much sense!" Aloud, he thanked the workman and added, "We passed the mail coach not long since. Best make room for it."

With awe, the man stepped back to allow Simon to turn his horses. "Passed mail coach, did'ee!"

With ease Simon turned his pair into the narrow lane and let them out at a moderate pace. The lane was narrow, and two carriages could not pass on it. Althea grew apprehensive. "Simon, are you sure this is the right way? This road might easily turn into someone's stableyard!"

"As a matter of fact, it does," said Simon easily. "Do you really not know where we are?"

"We did not cross the Lea," she said, and with returning spirit added, "And we are far behind that disgraceful couple. Surely we cannot gain on them on this—this cart track!"

"Not at all. We have them in our pocket."

"Simon, this is no time to make sport of me."

"My love, I shall never make sport of you!"

In a small voice, she protested, "I am not your love."

"No? That is a matter to be mended. But first we must deal with the matter at hand."

Studying him, she concluded, "You are no longer angry with them. In your pocket, of course you said so. I do understand that one of those curricles who must go this way around the bridge is Noel's, but how can you be sure we will come up with them? And what of the other curricle and the wagon? Shall we all arrive at the same stableyard? Really, Simon, I am vexed with you!"

"Truly? When I am more in charity with you than ever? I have merely realized what is important to me. You must overlook my happiness. I shall strive to please you, even if it means losing my temper again."

"You are quite beyond anything," she scolded. "Talking such nonsense when we are on a serious mission." In a moment curiosity overcame her, mingled, to be truthful, with a large portion of hope. "What *is* important to you?"

"We must discuss the subject at length." He shot

her a swift, appraising glance. "But you may be very sure the welfare of Lucy, or whoever she is, is a matter of vast indifference to me, now."

"But I feel obligated to get the girl back to Tom, intact and without harm done. After all, she is not a Rackham, but she is Lucy's cousin. We did accept her, you know. It is for Tom to say what is to become of her."

"You are right, of course. Where is Tom, do you think?"

"I have no idea. I thought he was at Darley Hall. I sent for him to come to Grosvenor Square, but that was before we learned that Eliz— It is so much easier to call her Lucy!"

"Then let us do so. I daresay she will not object at this late time. Before we learned that Lucy had forced Noel, the sapskull, to run off."

"I did not have time to write him again. Perhaps Bennie has sent him word of this development."

"And," said Simon with a smile, "perhaps she has not had time. Sir Horace may be renewing his suit at this very moment."

"Oh, I do hope so! Since the real Lucy is dead, then there is no reason for Bennie to refuse him again. But how can you suppose he would have called so early?"

"Did you not see him coming around the corner into the square just as we set forth? He gestured toward us, somewhat wildly as I thought, and I feared he would delay us badly."

"So you pretended not to see him?"

"I was in haste, as you recall, and I did not think you wished to tell him our tale in the street."

"Of course you were right." *As you usually are*, she thought, slightly irritated.

They rode along the lane, meeting no one but occasionally passing a wide place in the track, clearly constructed as lay-bys for accommodation of vehicles meeting on the narrow track. Althea felt her spirits returning, now that Simon seemed no longer in such haste to overcome the runaways and was thus not in apparent danger of losing his temper.

His resolution to avoid displays of anger lasted a very short time. The lane turned sharply and Simon did not slow for it, indeed acting very much like a man traveling along a road so familiar to him it might be his own. His speed was injudicious.

Just beyond the bend, the road was filled, stopped up completely. Instead of the narrow ruts formed by generations of wheeled travel, Althea saw the rounded woolly backs of newly shorn sheep. A hundred in the flock, at least, and she was sufficiently a country-woman to recognize that these sheep, far from being as docile as their kind was reputed to be, were agitated.

An overly excited ewe is unpredictable, and a hundred ewes in the same spirit are formidable.

"I see the shepherd, at the opening in the hedge," Althea pointed out.

"As do I," said Simon, "and what is more to the point, he sees us."

"Back away there," shouted the shepherd, waving his crook like a baton. "Do'ee let dogs go."

Sheep, since the twelfth century, had the right of way on narrow country roads. Althea knew the proper form to follow on meeting sheep, reared as she was on the Darley country estates the other side of the Lea, near Welwyn. One simply possessed one's soul in patience until the dogs could clear the sheep to one side of the road. In this instance, there was not sufficient room for curricle and sheep.

At the moment the flock was possessed of its own strong wish for independence. Newly shorn, as Althea had noted, they had experienced confining hands, the alarming experience of the shears running rapidly through the fleece, and the strange freedom when the heavy wool no longer hung about them. Ordinarily, ewes in particular submitted to this annual experience in ovine passivity, leaving any protest to the rams.

Remembering the workman's information—two

curricles and a wagon had turned into the lane before them—she realized the sheep had good reason to be bewildered. Reason or not, however, the barrier before them might as well have been a brick wall, for there was no way possible to go through, or around, the bleating, bobbing beasts.

The shepherd's intention was clear. He wished to move the sheep through the gap in the hedge, where he now stood, into the green pasture beyond. The sheep had not wished to turn into the field.

And Simon, fuming, holding his blacks in tight rein, backed them in a display of skill that would have brought roars of acclamation from any of his acquaintance. The shepherd merely glared.

At length the two busy dogs had rounded up their charges and funneled them with expert herding through the gap.

Simon moved the curricle ahead and stopped abreast of the shepherd. "Funston," said Simon in an equable tone, "you know the bridge on the high road is blocked. The mail coach may need to come this way."

"My lord," cried Funston, shocked. "I did not see who you was. Yon daft ones coming through like nobody else on the road is what did the damage."

"Are there any more flocks to come?"

"Nay, yon's the last on 'em. Good fleece this year too, so they say." He spoke in a country accent that was very nearly incoherent. Only someone tuned to country dialect could have understood him.

"My mother will be pleased," said Simon kindly, and lifted the reins.

Funston had not said his say. "Young Mr. Noel should 'a knowed better. But he flustered them ewes something fierce."

"I shall speak to him," promised Simon. Then, a thought occurring to him, he said, "There were two curricles—and a wagon. Did all go on through?"

"Some did," said the shepherd with a wise nod, "and some didn't."

Suppressing a windy sigh of resignation, Simon this time urged his pair ahead. Once under way, he glanced at Althea. "Did you understand him?"

"Of course, although some of the words he used are not in common use among our shepherds. The folk speech is almost like another language, isn't it?"

"A great deal of Saxon in it, handed down through the centuries. One wonders how the Normans dealt with what was literally a foreign tongue."

"Like they did all the rest," said Althea, "forced them to learn the language. I suppose, however, that farm folk were so unimportant that the Normans simply whipped understanding into them. Did Funston—you called him?—really not recognize you?"

"Shepherds can, in the ordinary way, see a gray wolf among gray rocks on a hillside more than a mile distant." He laughed. "He chose to make a mystery of it. But you will notice the sheep went through the gap in a hurry."

The lane was clear now and they made good speed. Although Simon had not explained precisely where they were, she knew they were on Halleck land. If his mother would be pleased at the quality of the fleece, then the Dowager Lady Halleck held, in all likelihood, a life interest in the estates they traversed at the moment.

"I thought you would figure it out," said Simon.

"How do you know I have?"

"My girl, I have studied your expressions for some years now. You have come to the conclusion that this country road goes through the small manor that my father left my mother for her comfort. If he had not, of course, I should have made adequate provision for her. This way, of course, she is quite independent." He thought a moment. "There will never be, however, anything of the dependent about my mother."

"I have met her only a few times, you know. Frankly, she terrifies me."

"Let us hope she has the same effect on our runaways."

They must be very near the drive that would lead to Lady Darley's home. In fact, she could discern in the distance the stone gates that flanked the entrance to the park. Suddenly apprehensive, she put her hand on Simon's arm.

"Don't worry, little love," he said caressingly. "She will not eat you up." In fact, the dressing down she had given him when she first heard that Althea no longer wanted him was one that would live in his memory. He dated the long, intense struggle, still not completely over, to master his temper from the day he stood on the carpet before her and listened to a reasoned sermon on his faults.

"We will have to deal with Noel and Lucy and send them back to town, and then," he promised, "I shall have something to say to you."

Her cheeks warmed. Truly she could barely wait to hear what he would say. Her hopes, always rising on the barest trifle, now had a more substantial foundation on which to soar.

They turned through the gates. The road itself went on, as she had learned. "Some went in, some went on." Noel, without doubt went in. The other curricle ahead of them as well as the wagon must have gone on.

The parkland, while not as extensive as that at Halleck Hall, was yet sufficient to provide a pleasant approach to the Queen Anne house of warm stone, imported from the Cotswolds, in which lived the Dowager Lady Halleck.

A glimpse through the gate of the stableyard at a distance—yes, the road did wind up in someone's stableyard!—showed her the curricle they had pursued all the way from London.

But then, surprised, she turned to Simon. "Did you see that? Which curricle is Noel's?"

"More to the point," suggested Simon grimly, "whose is the other one?"

22

Althea could not have, for her life, described the drawing room of the Dowager Lady Soames' manor house. But she could remember all her days the charged atmosphere that it contained as she stepped over the threshold.

Her swift glance took in young Lord Fabyan, standing at a window, his back turned ostentatiously to the company. Miss More was seated on a sofa, watching Noel with an anxious expression in her eyes.

Althea recognized Mr. Cosgrove, to her surprise, and remembered the second curricle in the stableyard. He must have been hard on the heels of the runaways, and while she could not fathom how he had learned of the elopement, she had a matter of urgency to deal with at once.

The dowager, in a chair set at right angles to the fireplace, looked over Althea's shoulder and recognized with mingled pleasure and relief that her son had come. She had become quite weary of these young people, and now she could see an end to the business.

Althea crossed to her. "Ma'am, I am sorry to intrude on your privacy with so little warning."

"My dear, I am pleased to see you. Perhaps now I may hope to be informed as to the truth of this matter. I confess I cannot understand anything my grandson has told me. I gather he is eloping to Gretna Green— with your niece, my dear? I cannot believe you have anything to do with such a havy-cavey scheme." Lady Soames took Althea's hand and looked searchingly into her face. "My dear Althea, I am so pleased to see you here in my home that I believe I could even forgive Noel his outrageous behavior."

"Thank you, ma'am," said Althea.

She scarcely knew where to start. First, however, she knew that she must deal with the young lady she still thought of as Lucy. She turned to her, ready to point out disgrace piled upon fraud, added to greedy ambition.

But Lucy was crumpled in a chair, in an attitude of the utmost despondency. She had not even looked up when Althea came into the room.

Althea went to her and put her hand on the girl's shoulder. "Elizabeth," she said in a low voice, "how can you have lent yourself to such a scheme? You must have known all would come out."

While Althea had not meant her words to carry beyond Lucy's ears, Noel had left the window and stood nearby. "Such a scheme indeed, Miss Rackham! I did all I could to dissuade her, but she insisted. Wanted to be wed at once."

"I daresay you did your best to dissuade her," said Althea reassuringly.

Noel had suffered wild swings of mood in the last few days sufficient to unsettle his manners, if not his mind. Deep circles under his eyes, trembling hands, spoke of a man tried beyond endurance.

Simon, speaking briefly to his mother, now came to stand beside Althea. It was past time, he deemed, to take a hand with young Noel. Apprised of the true identity of Miss Lucy and having no great confidence in his nephew's ability to extricate himself from the web in which he struggled, Simon cut ruthlessly to the core of the matter.

"Did you intend to go all the way to the border?"

"Of course not, Uncle. Why else did I come to Grandmama's?"

"And that, of course, explains how Mr. Cosgrove has found his way to this remote spot," Simon deduced. He turned to Claude. "As a matter of mere curiosity, I wonder just how he lured you into following him?"

"It is simple enough, my lord," said Mr. Cosgrove calmly. "He asked me to come to Netherton Magna. He said he was desperate. I required directions to that location and inquired of Miss More." He bowed slightly to Dorcas. "As a matter of fact, we never reached Netherton Magna. Perhaps I did not recognize the village?"

"When we could not cross the river," explained Dorcas, "I surmised that Noel must be planning to come to Lady Soames'."

"That explains everything," said Lady Soames, "except why this wretched boy was eloping in the first place. Surely he cannot want to marry the girl."

"She is so lovely," said Dorcas wistfully.

"I daresay," agreed the dowager. "Not the point. I agree one cannot give a Rackham a slip on the shoulder—" She was interrupted by a snort from Noel.

"That's just what she said I did," protested Noel. "She said she would tell everybody I tried to attack her that evening in Uncle Simon's house."

Lady Soames lifted an arched eyebrow at her son. "Good God, Simon, what kind of house do you run in London?"

"It was an accident, Mama," said Simon soothingly. In an altered tone he turned to Lucy. "You said yourself he fell and tried to catch his balance."

Lucy had spent her large store of defiance. She had been on tenterhooks for the weeks in London, striving to maintain an identity she understood only imperfectly. She had felt the urgency of time running out and saw Lord Fabyan as her only security. He was entranced by her beauty, as she had expected, but he jibbed at the last. Only by threatening to change her story about the accident was she able to persuade him to elope with her.

"I did not want to elope," she said now, huddled forlornly in her chair. "I should like to have had a great wedding, in St. Margaret's church, with all the *ton* there, seeing me."

Lady Soames expressed the thoughts of everyone. "Is that all?" she murmured ironically.

"That would have been enough," said Althea practically. She looked down at Lucy, her expression softening. The girl was miserable, and she sat unhappily in the shards of her dreams. The time had come for explanation. Nothing short of full revelation would serve. Noel must know the truth, and Mr. Cosgrove too. Dorcas had suffered from Lucy's deception and Lady Soames had been drawn into the tangle unwittingly.

Althea glanced at Simon, who nodded slightly. She could not have wished for a better audience. Five pairs of eyes were fixed on her. Only Lucy did not need to listen. She fixed her gaze on the floor, giving the impression that she had withdrawn from the company. She had no hope left.

"You see, Lady Soames," Althea began. "Lucy is not Lucy."

Noel stuttered, "N-not Lucy?" He glared accusingly at the girl. "Then who is she?"

"Her name is Elizabeth Osborne, Lucy's cousin. Lucy, the real Lucy, is dead. Elizabeth was her companion—"

She continued doggedly to the end of the story. "So when Lady St. Aubyn revealed to me what she knew of my niece, and it became clear to me that Lucy was Elizabeth—I cannot help but call her, even now, by my niece's name—of course I had to tell her she was discovered."

Simon added harshly, "My idiot nephew had put himself in an equivocal position, one that lent itself to blackmail."

Lady Soames, surprisingly, said, "Simon, pray ring

the bell for Willett. I feel the need of refreshment. Rather, restoratives."

With unerring good manners, the dowager had fixed upon the best way to ease the tension that had built up in the room. Not until Willett and a maid had brought in tea and stronger beverages did she revert to the topic that filled the minds of all.

"Althea, my dear, what a troubling time you must have had! I quite see your point. Who knows what any of us might have done if we had been left without friends or funds?"

"Blackmail, Mama?" said Simon quietly.

Lucy spoke for the first time since Althea and Simon had arrived. "It's easy enough for you to criticize, Lord Soames. You've never had to worry about your next meal, or where you could find to sleep. My father was a gentleman, and my mother's family was well-enough born, but that does not mean they had funds to leave me. Lucy Rackham was my only relative. Her mother and mine were cousins, and she asked me to come and live with her. Neither one of us had more than a handful of rupees to go on with, but together we could get by. And then the attorney wrote from London. He said she must come to England, to hear something, he said, to her advantage."

In her agitation, she rose and began to walk erratically around the room. Althea found it easy now to think of her as Elizabeth Osborne.

"He sent her funds for her ticket and enough extra so that we could scrape by if I called myself her maid and shared her cabin."

She stopped in her pacing and looked at them with haunted, desperate eyes. "And then Lucy got the plague and we missed the sailing. When she died, there was nowhere for me to go. Except to change the sailing reservation, which was in Lucy's name."

She fell silent. No one spoke. There was not a great deal that could be said. Abruptly, as though waking from sleep, she shook her head slightly. She curtsied to Lady Soames. "I am sorry to have caused you any trouble."

She crossed to stand before Althea. "You never liked me. I knew that. You were quite right, you see."

In complete silence she walked to the door, opened it, and disappeared into the hall, leaving a stunned group behind her.

Althea stirred. "It is true. She has caused a great deal of trouble and I felt I could never be fond of her. But I like her much better now."

Simon was looking from the window. "She cannot be allowed to go—"

Mr. Cosgrove rose, setting down his untouched whiskey. "Pray excuse me, Lady Soames," he said, incongruously formal in the circumstances, "I shall go after Miss—Miss Osborne." He explained to Althea, "While she is not the lady I was betrothed to, yet I think we may well suit. At least, I shall hope she will agree to accept my offer."

Simon looked at him with approval. "I suggest, Mr. Cosgrove, you do not linger here. Miss Osborne is already out of sight. If you take the drive to the right, you may overtake her."

For all his stockiness and his deliberate speech, Mr. Cosgrove was capable of a fine turn of speed when required. In only a few minutes, Simon announced, "He'll do."

From the drama unfolding on the driveway, he turned to a drama that had erupted in the drawing room. Oblivious to anyone else, Noel was kneeling before Dorcas, attempting to capture her hands.

"Dorcas, Dorcas, I never loved her."

"Truly, Noel?" she murmured.

"She was so beautiful and I admit I was fascinated. But at bottom, I knew I would come back to you."

"I could wish," said Dorcas in a clear, even voice, "that you had made me privy to your conviction."

He succeeded in catching hold of her hands. Enfolding them in his, he looked earnestly at her. "Can you forgive me, Dorcas? It was merely a kind of brainstorm."

Merely a brainstorm! thought Dorcas. He had broken their engagement, defied his mother, treated Dorcas herself so badly that she would never forget the hurt, and so conducted himself as to be vulnerable to blackmail in the form of a forced elopement.

It was not due to any elevated scruples that he had brought Lucy—Miss Osborne—to his grandmother. His note to Claude Cosgrove, a man he scarcely knew, imploring help, had given her much food for thought.

"Can you?" Noel repeated in an agonized tone.

"Forgive you?" repeated Dorcas. She had, to her surprise, enjoyed the past weeks in London, under the sponsorship of her aunt Lady Barnett. Young Lord Fabyan was far from being the only eligible gentleman in town. With a delicious sense of freedom, of burden lifted, of yoke removed, she said very gently, "I do not think so, Noel."

She caught Simon's eye on her and read approval in it. She smiled, a curious smile of release and anticipation. Life was going to be better, she knew—it could hardly be worse than it had been.

Noel's expression was all that any vindictive young lady could desire. Dorcas withdrew her hands and said with real sympathy, "Pray do not look so, Noel. You will find someone who will suit. I shall expect to see an announcement of our failed betrothal in the *Gazette*."

Noel got to his feet. He was not sure what had happened to him. His whole purpose only weeks ago was to divest himself of an unwanted betrothal. Now, stunned, his wish was granted, and he did not like it above half.

"I suppose you will allow me to take you to your home?" he suggested. "London is too far to travel before dark."

Simon intervened. "Quite ineligible, Noel. Miss More does not deserve to be burdened with your company. Dear Mama, may I ask the loan of your carriage? Althea and I will see that Dorcas is safely restored to her father."

"Of course."

Althea, from embarrassed avoidance of the painful scene that was unfolding between Noel and Dorcas, had gone to gaze unseeing from the window looking out on the drive.

A startling sight appeared before her. Her own traveling coach and four, John on the box, came rolling up the drive to stop before the entrance. Samuel dropped to the ground and let down the steps. She recognized with sinking heart the figure that emerged from the vehicle and started purposefully toward the front door.

"Good God, Simon," she cried faintly, "it's Tom!"

23

Simon was at her side in two strides.

"In your coach? What does he mean?"

"I sent for him yesterday, you know. I cannot think how he can have thought to come here."

She turned to Lady Soames and cried, "How much you must dislike having all this—this trouble dropped on you! And it's all my fault!"

"My dear," said Lady Soames bracingly, "the only thing you ever did that I disliked was when you cast off my son. And that was not your fault. I myself should not have wished to live with him—then." She smiled sweetly at her son. "You know that is true, Simon."

"Indeed I do," he said stiffly. "I believe it was then that you decided to remove to this house?"

"And you must admit we have gone on much more comfortably. But perhaps there has been some alteration—"

"Mama," said Simon harshly, "pray do not plead my case. I suspect we will have plenty to do just now in pacifying Lord Darley. He gave every sign on his way to the door of a man ready to erupt like a volcano."

Simon had the right of it. Willett had barely time to announce Lord Darley before that nobleman was in the room.

With excellent manners, Tom ignored the others in the room for the moment. He crossed to Lady Soames.

"I trust I see you well, ma'am. I apologize for intruding on your privacy, but my errand is sufficiently urgent to be my excuse."

Lady Soames had experienced more excitement this day than in any day in the past ten years. She had resigned herself to living, even though most comfortably, in an undisputed backwater, far from the best traveled roads and removed from society. But today she had entertained an eloping couple, who were quite definitely not stirred by passion; an Irishman whom she had never seen before; lovely Dorcas, who seemed to have come to her senses and refused Lady Soames' own grandson—a good day's work, she considered it.

It looked, moreover, as though Simon had mended his fences with Althea. Although neither of them was aware of it, the glances that passed between them were telling, not to say languishing. Of the six young people in the room, only her son and his former fiancée were truly enamored of each other. Lady Soames believed she could rest easy on that head.

And now came Tom Darley, roaring like a lion blocked from his prey, a fairly intelligent man who had married a woman entirely unsuitable for him.

Lady Soames was becoming amused. More activity here than in Bond Street, she thought. She was thus able to greet Lord Darley with a smile and a word of genuine welcome.

"Your errand?" she prompted him.

He was glaring around the room. "There you are, Althea," he blurted. "What are you doing here? I should like to know what kind of a house you run in Grosvenor Square!"

Simon made a move as though to intervene, but a small gesture from Althea stayed him. She said reprovingly, "Tom, Lady Soames may take offense at your tone. And right. I should not like to hear you speak so crudely in my own drawing room."

"Crude! I warrant you, what I saw in your drawing room passes everything!"

Lady Soames, now moved by the same sense of humor that often visited her son, said, "Lord Darley, pray tell us what you saw in dear Althea's drawing room! My own, you must know, is rarely exciting."

"A pair of them," Tom answered, moderating his voice in deference to the age of his hostess. "A middle-aged pair, locked in what I can only call a disgraceful embrace. Embracing, right there in public."

"Tom, that cannot be true! In public? You told us, my drawing room, which is hardly a place of common resort."

"I saw 'em, didn't I?" Tom pointed out with an air of reasonableness. "Never thought it of Bennie."

"Oh, good," exclaimed Althea. "You were right, Simon. Bennie and Sir Horace, I suppose?"

Tom stared at her. "You know about this?"

"I do not know, Tom, I only hoped."

"What will you do if Bennie leaves you? I suppose Wychley means marriage. You cannot stay in Grosvenor Square alone. I won't have it."

"Darley—"

"Never mind, Simon. I have matter of my own to speak to my brother about. Lady Soames, is there a place where we can be private?"

Following her own wish not to be excluded from what promised to be an exciting dialogue, she said, "I'm sorry, my dear. My house is so small—"

Simon's breath exploded in a short word. "Fustian!" No one heeded him.

Tom was well away. "What is this urgent matter you sent for me about? I collect it pertains to my niece Lucy." He looked around the room again. "I expected to find her here. Where is she? What is this all about?"

"About Lucy, as I told you," began Althea. She was by now heartily weary of the entire matter, but the story must be told again.

"I do not precisely know," Althea answered literally. "When we saw her last—"

"Caroline told me you couldn't be trusted with a young lady."

"Then," said Simon, ignoring Althea's frantic gesture, "I wonder that Lady Darley did not accept the responsibility, which is without question hers? If she had, all these unfortunate happenings would have been avoided."

Struck by a note in Simon's voice, Tom halted. "You mean that, Soames? I don't see how. Lucy is Althea's niece, not Caroline's."

"You quibble," said Simon warningly.

"The trouble is," Althea rushed into explanation, "Lucy is—not Lucy."

Lady Soames thought it was time to intervene. "Althea dear, you must tell your brother before he has an apoplectic fit. Lord Darley, do sit down, there. Your presence is becoming quite uncomfortable to me."

Reluctantly, Tom sat where his hostess indicated. He said to his sister, "Very well. I do not know what maggot you've got in your head, but I'm willing to listen."

Simon murmured, "You'd better," but fortunately Tom did not hear him.

"Now, Tom, pray do not interrupt me with foolish questions. I promise you I shall not leave anything out. I have told the tale often enough to be letter-perfect. To begin with, Lucy is dead."

Tom stared at her. He sputtered. "Thought you said you didn't know where she was?"

"Tom, please listen for once in your life. I shall not blame you in the least, but you must hear the story, at once." So admonishing him, she continued. He kept a praiseworthy silence, although more than once his effort to restrain himself was visible.

"So there it is," finished Althea. She had labored for some weeks at a task she found distasteful, one that was not properly hers to do. Usually one to overlook the injustices her family visited on her—as Simon had pointed out, at length and more than once—she had come to the belief that resistance was desirable. Tom had given every indication of forbidding her to live in Grosvenor Square, in her own house, using her own funds, if Bennie were to marry and move away.

Althea realized that she could not rely on Tom's complacence on her behalf. Nor did she wish to enlist Simon on her side, not after their long-ago quarrels, not when her own feelings about him were so overpowering. She clamped the lid on her strong desire to permit Simon to protect her and speak for her.

This was something she must do for herself.

"There it is," growled Tom. "You say the girl is out in the woods here? With that Irish feller right behind her? I wonder you allowed it."

"There was no question of allowing it, Tom," said Althea firmly. "You gave our niece into my charge. Elizabeth Osborne has no connection with me. It is you and Mr. Dedman who have brought the girl to England. It is you and Mr. Dedman who will determine what is to be done with her."

Lady Soames and her son exchanged glances full of meaning. Althea at last was standing on her own feet. Tom stared at her in disbelief. "B-but, Althea, Caroline cannot take the girl in. Especially when she isn't even a Rackham!"

"Then, Tom, I suggest that Caroline examine her duties more carefully. You are the head of the family. And whether or not Elizabeth Osborne goes to Darley Hall, or directly to Ireland, with or without marriage, is no longer a concern of mine."

"Althea!"

"But I tell you this, Tom. Elizabeth will not return to Grosvenor Square."

Tom gazed inwardly, apparently at the prospect of conveying Althea's message to his wife, and shied. In a more temperate manner, he suggested, "But with Bennie gone you will have more time—"

"Thomas," said Althea sternly, "I recommend you forget any scheme for bringing the girl back to me. I will not have her."

Althea had entirely forgotten that Dorcas and Noel were still in the room. With surprise she realized that they were both riveted.

Tom opened his mouth to speak. She must forestall him, and most happily was visited by inspiration. "Dorcas must be taken home, Tom. I suggest that you take Elizabeth to Darley Hall, and Dorcas may go on then to her father's, since London is too far to go tonight. You may," she concluded generously, "use my coach and my servants."

Althea had begun to shake. The emotions to which she had just given voice drained away, leaving her spent. She believed she had solved her problems—Elizabeth was off her hands and Tom had been warned away from her own life. She felt purged. She also felt uncomfortably weak.

She dared not look at Simon, lest he be tempted to add his exhortations and accusations to hers. She was going to be sick, she needed air, she might faint. She crossed the room swiftly and went to the front door. The well-trained footman reached it before her and she did not need even to hesitate before she was across the threshold and into the open air.

Elizabeth had gone, Simon had said, along the driveway to the right. Automatically, she turned to the left. Walking briskly, hoping to get beyond view of the house before she succumbed to the nausea roiling in her stomach, she was soon hidden by the great trees of the park.

The exertion of a few deep breaths made her feel better, and in a little while she was past the danger of violent illness.

She walked for a long time, slowing eventually and remembering her inexcusable rudeness to Lady Soames. The dowager had been much put upon by the influx of quarrelsome and lovelorn and outrageous visitors, and Althea had added to the sum by walking out without so much as a word.

She must go back, and quickly.

Someone stood in the drive some little distance behind her. She uttered a faint shriek of alarm before she recognized him. Simon advanced more quickly now.

"I did not hear you behind me."

"I feared to frighten you," he explained.

The small silence that fell between them was excessively unsettling to her. As he drew nearer, she could see the unwonted seriousness of his expression, the queer hungry look in his amber eyes.

"S-Simon," she said softly.

"My dear, I told you I would have a question to ask you when this mess was cleared away. I think you know what it is?"

She did not precisely know, but she hoped very hard. She began to tremble again. Dreading him to see her so unnerved, she burst into speech. "Simon, I beg of you to consider. You wish a docile bride. I would try to be more biddable, but, alas, Simon, you know I cannot be other than I am."

"I have not asked you to alter for me."

He did not want her! He did not care enough even to listen to her protests. He did not intend to offer for her!

The tears started behind her eyelids. She looked away, unable to still the quivering of her lips. She was no better than Elizabeth, who leapt to accept offers that had not been made.

She drew a quick little gasping breath. She must get back to the house before she quite dissolved in weeping. She took only one step before she found herself up against his hard chest, his strong arms holding her safe from escape, even had she wanted to pull away.

"You little idiot," he said fondly. "Do you think—could you *possibly* have thought—I should want a biddable bride?"

She sniffed and found a large handkerchief in her hand. "You told me so."

In a voice she had heard once before, he said, "Of all the things I have said, you must choose the most palpable lie to believe."

She gave him a watery smile and lifted her gaze to his. "Not docile, then?"

Seized with belated caution, he amended, "Not unruly, my dear, but—spirited, lively, mischievous, utterly adorable—yes, yes, yes!"

His answer was entirely satisfactory, as was his immediate possession of her lips. She gave herself up to the emotion she had stifled two years before. It had come back, she thought in a kind of delirium, stronger than she could have believed.

Neither of them heard the footsteps approaching. They did not hear Lord Darley's muttered oath as he caught sight of his sister locked in an embrace in public.

"My own sister!" he exploded. He turned on his heel to return to the house. As he walked with lengthening stride, his spirits rose.

I can't handle her anymore, he told himself. Maybe Soames can tame her! Can't say I envy him!

At that moment, Simon released his dear love long enough to tender the olive branch he had been nurturing for almost two years. "Darling, I'll forgive you your family," he began.

Instant retort sprang to her lips, but the words were never spoken. For Simon went on to add, "If you will forgive me mine."

"You have expressed exactly my sentiments," she told him with a smile.

He put his finger under her chin and lifted her face to his. "Speaking of sentiment," he said, and spoke no more.

She thought, however, that actions, which are supposed to speak louder than words, left nothing wanting.

About the Author

Vanessa Gray grew up in Oak Park, Illinois, and graduated from the University of Chicago. She currently lives in the farm country of northeastern Indiana, where she pursues her interest in the history of Georgian England and the Middle Ages. She is the author of a number of bestselling Regencies—*The Masked Heiress, The Lonely Earl, The Wicked Guardian, The Wayward Governess, The Dutiful Daughter, The Innocent Deceiver, The Reckless Orphan,* and *The Duke's Messenger*—available in Signet editions.

JOIN THE *REGENCY ROMANCE* READERS' PANEL

Help us bring you more of the books you like by filling out this survey and mailing it in today.

1. Book Title: _____

   Book #: _____

2. Using the scale below, how would you rate this book on the following features? Please write in one rating from 0-10 for each feature in the spaces provided.

POOR		NOT SO GOOD			O.K.			GOOD		EXCEL-LENT
0	1	2	3	4	5	6	7	8	9	10

RATING

Overall opinion of book .... _____
Plot/Story .... _____
Setting/Location .... _____
Writing Style .... _____
Character Development .... _____
Conclusion/Ending .... _____
Scene on Front Cover .... _____

3. About how many romance books do you buy for yourself each month? _____

4. How would you classify yourself as a reader of Regency romances?
   I am a ( ) light ( ) medium ( ) heavy reader.

5. What is your education?
   ( ) High School (or less) ( ) 4 yrs. college
   ( ) 2 yrs. college   ( ) Post Graduate

6. Age _____   7. Sex: ( ) Male ( ) Female

Please Print Name_____

Address_____

City _____ State _____ Zip _____

Phone # ( )_____

Thank you. Please send to New American Library, Research Dept., 1633 Broadway, New York, NY 10019.